Extinct

By TP Hogan

NATIONAL
LIBRARY
OF AUSTRALIA

A catalogue record for this
book is available from the
National Library of Australia

Acknowledgements

To the awesome people who helped me with my research:
- Caz from Cooloola Tattoo, Gympie – who agreed to be interviewed about what it is like to own and run a tattoo parlour. You gave me so much more than I could use in this story, and I thank you.
- The unknown staff behind the help button at the Tasmanian Museum and Art Gallery who provided material and answered questions about thylacine and sarcophagus harrisii

To the readers who kept asking for the next book, and keeping me motivated.

And of course to my husband, who sat through copious documentaries and patiently taught me how to (finally) pronounce 'Thylacine'.

Authors Note

This story is set in Australia with Australian characters. The spelling and grammar is Australian English.

A glossary of Australian terminology used in this story is provided at the back of this book.

Titles by TP Hogan

Nephilim Code

Nova
Edward
Zeph

—

Shattered

—

Extinct

Escape...and explore hidden worlds.

www.tphogan.com

Chapter One

Pretending to be normal was hard when I was seeing things. And I had to be seeing things. There was no way a silver dog-like creature was silently padding its way across the black-and-white checker tiled floor of the tattoo parlour. The edges of its shape were blurred, a ghostly mist, and it walked with no sound. No click of nails, no panting of breath. Through its ethereal form, the black section of floor paled charcoal grey. Black pool eyes bore into mine as if it could see into my soul and it was slightly amused by what it saw.

Barely breathing, I stared down at it. My head was starting to pound with every heartbeat. I was half expecting it to fling itself at me without warning, ferociously snapping its jaws. After all, wasn't that what ghosts did? After standing all silent and eerie, they did a sudden jump attack.

This one didn't attack. It yawned its long, slender snout with wide gaping jaws and far too many sharp teeth. It was like no type of dog I'd ever seen. Its body was sleek and long, ending in a stiff tail that reached the floor, and it had stripes like black claw marks ripping across its back.

"May I help you?"

My head spun around toward the sound of the voice and it took a second before I saw the woman behind the counter. The light blue and bright red of her cherry-covered fifties pin-up dress dazzled after the watery silver of the ghost dog. Her jet-black hair cut into a short, sharp bob only accentuated the swirl of coloured ink down her left arm, from shoulder to wrist. She was looking at me with a blink of blue eyes, a pleasant smile, and an expectant glance. She was looking directly at me and not reacting in the slightest to the ghost in the middle of her tattoo parlour. Although her friendly smile was starting to waver at the edges and I was pretty sure she was starting to think I could be a person to be wary of.

I took another look at the dog. It stood there, motionless. I moved a step away. It stayed. I took another and another, and it merely watched me. If it stayed exactly where it was, I could probably attempt to ignore it.

"Um… hi." Moving my backpack up my arm and out of the way, I shoved my hand out for a handshake. Not smooth at all. "My name is Ginny Martin."

"How can I help you?"

"I hope you can help me." Struggling with my bag, I pulled my portfolio out of the depths. I should have had it out in the first place. It would have looked more organised. "I'm looking for an apprenticeship."

"You are?" She sounded cautious, and the silver dog lifted its head.

I kept it in my sight as I held out the portfolio

she didn't take. The dog stayed in the same spot and I felt foolish standing there, still holding the matte-black binder. Trying to ignore the dog, I placed the portfolio on the counter and opened it to the first page, hoping she'd take notice.

"My dad said I could quit school if I got a job. I went to the guidance counsellor at school, and all she had was apprenticeships for a chef and a mechanic. But she said if I could get a business to agree to take me on, she'll do all the paperwork for the apprenticeship. And you can do an apprenticeship for a tattoo artist. I looked it up." I gulped a breath to try to stop my babbling and turned a page on the portfolio, hoping she'd look down at the drawings.

"I'm sorry. I can't help you. I'm not in the position to take anyone on."

I took a step back as the sliver dog planted its stance. I was pretty sure it was going to start growling in a second.

Clearing my throat, I took another half step away and pointed at the page again. "At least look at the—"

"Sorry."

Without another word, she moved away from the counter and disappeared behind a door that read *Staff Only*, leaving it swinging silently in her wake and me standing near the counter with a hackle-raised ghost dog between me and the front door. Its eyes never left me, and I could hear the hollow *swick* of the clock snatching the seconds between us. Only three or four of them sounded in the silence, but it was an eternity before the dog lowered its gaze. A moment later, it unexpectedly relaxed, gave me one last look, and silently slid *through* the closed staff door. My heart jerked into a pounding tempo and I closed my eyes. This couldn't be real. It wasn't possible. Shaking my head, I opened my eyes. The door was still closed. The dog was gone. It hadn't been a Drawing image. I'd never seen a Drawing image move, for starters.

Someone spoke behind me.

I jumped and spun. He wasn't much older than me, but he was taller. And I couldn't help but appreciate the fine muscular build filling out his long-sleeved shirt and jeans. His sandy brown hair spilled down to touch his shoulders as he turned to place his shucked jacket and motorbike helmet on one of the hooks near the counter. Flicking a hair tie from his wrist, he tied back his hair, turned to me, and smiled. It was a nice smile.

"Sorry, I didn't mean to scare you. Is someone helping you?"

I saw movement out the corner of my eye and slowly turned my head. The silver dog was back, watching me. As much as I wanted a tattoo artist apprenticeship, I didn't want it badly enough to put up with ghost dogs.

"I'm fine, thanks. I was leaving. Now. Thanks."

The cold hit me full blast as I almost ran from the shop, instantly freezing my fingers and cutting through my open jacket. Struggling to zip it up, I power walked down the street. I didn't want to stop long enough to win the battle with the tiny silver tag, so I jammed the jacket closed around me, crossed my arms over the fabric, and nearly broke into a run in my need to put distance between me and the Painted Serpent. Gasping for air, I made it to the bus stop without encountering another ghost dog. The girl sitting in the shelter gave me a sideways look as I pulled up in an abrupt jerk and made a show of looking at the timetable, feeling like an idiot. At any second, I expected the ghost dog to appear, but it didn't. And there should not be any reasonable expectation for it to do so.

Ever.

I didn't know what the hell that was. I'd never seen anything like it before in my life, and I never wanted to see it again.

A low-pitched growl behind me made me jump and stumble three steps backwards before the hiss of brakes and the hulking shape confirmed the arrival of the bus. My hands shook so much I nearly couldn't get my money out for the ticket, and I was glad the other girl went first. It gave me enough time to pull myself together. Collapsing into the nearest seat, I laid my head against the cold glass of the window.

Safe.

The world looked normal. Cars switched their headlights on against the darkening sky. Lights from buildings and street lamps spilled into the street and reflected in the cold misty air. People huddled in jackets and, puffing mists of air with their breaths, darted in and out of cars and shops. It was a normal Friday evening. Ghosts didn't exist. It was impossible. I must have dreamed it, or something.

I changed buses and watched the sky as night crept in. Night came faster here. The further from town the bus travelled, the calmer I became. Dad's house was the last one in Queenstown on the way out to Zeehan near the Yolande River. The bus route didn't go all the way out there. Stepping off at the last stop, I went into the yard of the house behind the bus stop and unhooked my bike.

"Evening, Ginny."

I looked up then waved at the lady in the old fashioned floral dress, wrapped in a bulky puke-green padded jacket with Ugg boots disappearing under her hem. She stood at her front door holding the teapot she'd emptied onto the plants, and I was pretty sure she'd held on to that pot of old tea until she'd seen the bus pull up.

"Hi, Mrs Milligan."

"Running late today?"

"Had an appointment in town after school."

"I'll get Steve to toss your bike into the back of the ute. You don't have a light on that thing. You'll get cleaned up for sure."

If it meant getting a lift home, I wasn't about to argue. I'd only been riding the bike for two weeks, and the ten kilometres a day was nearly killing me. At least I was getting to the point where my legs wanted to move the next day.

I was unceremoniously shooed to sit in the old pale blue ute while Mr Milligan set about getting my bike tied down in the tray. He thumped the tailgate twice which seemed to be the signal for Mrs Milligan to start the wheezing and scarily shuddering engine. She turned the knob for the heater, but I didn't hold much hope for any heat from the tiny vents. The ute was decorated with rust and held together with what looked like duct tape and bits of wire. When she turned the key, it coughed like a ninety-year-old, four-pack-a-day smoker, and going by the black cloud of exhaust fumes, my estimation might not have been too far off.

"How's your dad doing?" Mrs Milligan turned down the radio as we travelled.

I shrugged. "Fine, I guess."

"The two of you getting on okay?"

I shrugged again, this time blinking to clear my vision. This was all I needed right now.

"Must be a huge change." She tried again.

"Yeah."

"Made any new friends yet?"

"Not yet."

I wished she'd stop talking and turn the radio back on or something. It was hard to focus on what she was saying. This one had hit me unusually fast. Hiding my left hand between my leg and the door, I wiggled my fingers. Sometimes that helped. It worked. My vision cleared a little. I took a slow breath in and kept wiggling my fingers until Mrs Milligan drove down the dirt road to the front of Dad's house.

"Well, there we go, love."

"Thanks, Mrs Milligan."

Together we took the bike out of the tray and I breathed a sigh of relief as her car crunched its way down the drive, wheezing and coughing exhaust fumes until it was out of sight. I scrabbled in my backpack for the garage remote then wheeled the bike inside, dropping it down against the wall without even kicking the stand out. I didn't have a key to the front door, and the garage was the only way in unless I felt like rummaging in the woodshed for the spare key. I didn't have time for that now. I still had to navigate around Dad's workspace and all his equipment before I could get into the house. Flicking my hand was only clearing my head enough to stumble into my room and fumble for the nearest sketchpad and pencil. The image of the dog was still blurring my vision, and it wouldn't leave until I had it down on paper. I called it my 'Drawing image' and it only showed up when it wanted to be drawn. No one understood what I meant by that and I didn't tell too many people. I didn't need it added to the list of things that classified me as "crazy."

The image floated in front of my eyes like a yellow and pink veil until I looked down at a white page. When I did, it became a black-and-white image floating above the paper, sinking down like rivers of ink until I drew. With each line drawn, a little of the image would disappear. When I drew, I wasn't making it up. I was seeing it. Then my hand drew what I saw. Everyone told me drawing was hard. It wasn't.

This time, the silver dog floated above the page.

Yawning.

Padding across the floor.

Glaring at me.

Image after image. I nearly couldn't keep up. At some point, I switched on my lamp and the light splashed across the page, highlighting the graphite smudging my fingers. Eight pages were completely full of sketches and the damn dog was finally out of my head. I sat back against the chair with a slow exhale and shook then flexed my left hand. It ached and burned, but it was something I was used to. I picked up a page and studied the animal. It was the strangest dog I'd ever seen. It looked bloody feral. I was surprised the woman and the guy hadn't reacted. Maybe they were used to it. Or maybe they didn't see it. I slammed the book shut. It was only a strange dog. I draw strange things all the time, what I'd seen in the floating images. I took a breath and stood from my chair.

"You're normal. Just a normal kid. Going through life."

Breathing deeply and as slowly as I could, I focused on the scratches on my desktop. I'd opted for a single bed so I could fit both desks into the room—my homework desk and my drawing desk. The drawing desk was one of my favourite things. It was a full-sized drafting desk I'd picked up for thirty dollars at the dump shop back home. It was scratched and dinted, old, and ratty, but it was mine. As my fingers bumped softly over the grooves, and the last coils of fear dissipated with the hypnotic motion, I became aware of the distant sound of voices. Still flexing my hand, I went into the kitchen.

Spaghetti was cooking on the stove alongside some heavenly smelling sauce and mince. I gave the sauce a quick stir and snuck a taste.

"Dad?" It still felt weird calling him that.

"In here."

I followed the sound of his voice into the living room, where he sat in front of the TV in one of only two armchairs in the room. Two tattered brown fabric armchairs, one chipboard coffee table, one lamp with no shade, one brown Laminex cabinet at the other end of the room with the TV and stereo, a clock that I couldn't decide if it was cool or kitsch, and a built-in mantle above the fireplace. That was the complete listing of the obviously second-hand furniture in the lounge room. I had more stuff in my room than he had in the entire house, if the garage wasn't included. He took minimalism to the extreme, but I think it had more to do with the fact he was male and didn't do house decorating type stuff than any need for peace or Zen.

"When did you get home?" I sat in the second La-Z-Boy, which, by default, had become "mine."

"About an hour ago. I said hello, but you didn't look up."

"I didn't hear you." I pointed toward the kitchen. "I stirred the sauce."

"Thanks."

"You shouldn't leave it, you know. It'll burn."

"I've got the timer on. I'll check it when it beeps."

He kept looking at me. Waiting for the next brilliant piece of conversation, no doubt. I had nothing. After a while, he went back to watching the news on TV. I'd been drawing for about three hours according to the clock on the mantle. Mum would have never let me get away with drawing for the extra hour after she got home. She certainly wouldn't have made dinner without making me get up and help. I would have had to help the second she walked in the door. Some changes I could totally deal with. My fingers tapped against the brown padded arm of the chair. Despite the announcer on the TV, the quiet was getting on my nerves a little bit. Back home, it was always noisy. Six girls in one house had a lot to do with that. I always craved peace and quiet. Now that I had it, it felt completely wrong.

"How was work?" I asked Dad, attempting to fill the silence.

"All right. Cornelia made cupcakes. I hid one in the fridge for you but forgot to bring it home. Some bugger will have eaten it by tomorrow."

"That's okay." I kicked out the footrest and swung the handle at the side of the chair to keep it in place. "Thanks for the thought."

"How about you? Going to school on Monday?"

"Looks like it."

"Did you try the tattoo place?"

My heart skipped a beat then raced to make it up. "Yeah."

"No joy?"

"Nope."

"Well, you can't win 'em all, kiddo. Something will come along." He gave a quick smile in my direction before turning back to the news.

I watched him for a little while. He was so different to how I'd thought he'd be. For starters, he had a beard. The two photos Mum had of him showed him clean-shaven. Secondly, I thought he'd be all disciplinarian on my arse. After all, Mum sent me here to "straighten me out." So far, he was pretty laid back. He had a couple of rules. Text him if I was going to be late, and let him know where I'd be. Also, I had to keep my part of the house clean. Bedroom, bathroom, lounge room, and foyer was "my" part. Plus, mow the lawn on the opposite fortnight to him. He got his room, the kitchen, dining room, and laundry.

As far as I was concerned, he got the bad end of the deal.

Leaning back in the chair, I watched the TV for a bit.

"...found a dead body. Police have..."

I was surprised when I saw Dad in his green Ranger's uniform crossing behind the news reporter on the screen.

"Hey, that's you."

"Yeah."

"You were involved in a murder?"

"Some hikers called in that they found the body."

There was no way I was expecting that. "A dead body. That's bitchin'."

"Ginny." He frowned at me.

"What?"

"A person is dead. A person with family. A person who won't come home today."

"Sorry. It's just I didn't expect…. Do you have to deal with that kind of thing often?"

"No, thank God. And if you don't mind, I'd love it if we changed the subject."

"Change subject?" I nodded. "I can do that. Does Mum know you're letting me quit school?"

Dad dropped his head onto the back of his chair. I was pretty sure there was some eye rolling going on there. "You haven't quit, yet. When you actually get a job, I'll let her know."

"Why are you letting me do this?"

"Look for a job?"

"Quit."

He muted the sound then bounced the remote in his hand as he spoke. "Two suspensions last year. Doesn't sound like you really want to be there."

"You know she's going to have a fit."

Pressing his lips together, Dad gave a slow nod. "Yep."

"She'll yank me back to Townsville. Is that your plan?"

"No. I got through high school by the skin of my teeth. You're intelligent, but not all of us are designed to fit in the restricted school environment. Get your feet wet, decide where you want to focus, and who knows? You may finish high school yet."

I was not expecting that. "You know she thinks

a university education is the be all and end all, right?"

"I know."

"I'll be on the next flight back. You watch."

"Is that what you want?"

I frowned. In all the screaming matches with Mum and all the mess in being pulled up from everything I've ever known and thrust into the colder climes of the unknown to live with a man I didn't remember ever meeting, this was the first time anyone had asked what I wanted. Two weeks ago, I would have jumped at the chance to go back, but that was before he'd given me the offer to quit school. Back home, I'd be right back into that green-and-white checked uniform before I'd had the chance to unpack.

"I don't know."

"Not quite the end of the earth here, hey?" he teased, mocking my quote from the first day I'd arrived.

I laughed. "No, not quite. But if I stand on the shore, I can see it from here."

"Ha, ha." Dad threw the cushion from the chair at me as the timer for the spaghetti went off. "Just for that, you can check on dinner."

It was weird how smoothly dinner went. He plated up, we ate, I rinsed the dishes and stacked the dishwasher, and he cleaned up the rest of the kitchen. Meal done. There was no screaming, no crying or fighting, no demands for different food or squabbles over whose turn it was to clean up.

Almost eerie.

"You want to watch the movie with me?" Dad slid the tea towel over the handle of the oven. "It's *Gladiator*."

I didn't know the movie. I did have homework, but it was Friday night. "Is it any good?"

"A bit of 'beat 'em up, bash 'em up' mindless entertainment. You don't have to sit through the whole thing if you don't want to, but at least give it a chance."

"Sure, why not?"

"Great. Close the curtains in the lounge room, while I make up a cuppa. What breed of your four thousand herbal teas do you want?"

"Peach, and there's only seven flavours in there and some of them are infusions."

"Mm-hmm. Could have fooled me."

Grinning at his mumbling, I crossed the dingy grey carpet to the windows. The house had magnificent character features on the outside but was washed out on the inside. Pale grey carpets, yellow-cream walls, and wood trim. Oh, so imaginative. Dad's lack of decorating didn't help matters—a feature clock on the mantle sculpted to show Ned Kelly's last stand, notwithstanding.

As I reached window number three, Dad switched off the light and flicked on the lamp between the armchairs. In that moment of darkness, I could have sworn I saw something outside. Moving closer to the window, I cupped my hands against the glass and peered out to the driveway. With a gasp, I stepped back.

"What's wrong?"

I pointed at the window as I turned to look at him. "Do you see that? On the driveway?"

"See what?" He moved until he stood beside me and peered out the window. "I can't see anything."

Shielding the light, I took a second look. It was

still there. The ghost dog had followed me home. "You can't see anything?"

"No. Why? What am I supposed to be seeing?"

Licking my lips, I swallowed. It was standing barely inside the beam from the outside house light, clear as anything. It wasn't doing anything other than standing there.

"Nothing." I cleared my throat and took a deliberate step back. "Must have been a reflection or something."

"Okay. Your tea's ready, and the movie is about to start."

Hurriedly, I pulled the heavy brown curtain closed, blocking out all view of outside, and nearly raced for the armchair. Dad hadn't seen it. It was my childhood all over again. When I didn't know to keep my mouth shut about the Drawing images I saw. Two years of visiting shrinks certainly fixed that for me. The Drawing images I knew. I could recognise when I was seeing those. I could tell by the slight heaviness in the back of my head. This was completely different. This had no tell-tale side effect. I was seeing the dog along with everything else. A part of the real world. This time, I knew better than to open my mouth about it. The only thing I didn't know was how to stop it from following me.

Chapter Two

Shivering, I huddled into myself as I walked between the red brick school buildings. It was easy to spot the locals. They were the ones walking around in short-sleeved school uniforms. Not me. I still had my jumper on. The wind blew through the school and took a short cut right through me, an icy knife that sent shivers and goose bumps running all over my body. Reaching the English classroom, I was relieved to see some of the others already in there. Waiting for Mr Goss in the comfort of the classroom was a much better idea than braving the wind tunnel outside.

The room was set up so the desks formed a horseshoe shape around the outside of the room with three long forward-facing desks in the middle. The centre desks were already half full, so I made my way towards the back of the room, scooting around the right arm of the horseshoe and trying not to smack anyone in the head with my armful of books. They all talked amongst themselves, although I received one wave from a girl with short blonde hair, sitting at one of the centre tables. Evie, I think her name was. I gave her a small wave in return then sank down in my seat. She leaned back, swinging a little on her chair so she could get closer.

"Hi, I'm Evie."

"Ginny."

"You're new."

Lifting my eyebrows, I didn't answer. It was pretty obvious.

She gave me another smile, tapped her fingers on the desk, and then dropped her chair back down to talk to the girl who had turned around from the desk in front of her to ask her something. I breathed a sigh of relief. Someone who acknowledged I existed. That was nice, but not particularly wanted. Not in English class. This was one class I wanted to remain invisible.

The room wasn't much warmer than outside, and I huddled in the chair, trying to warm my hands. It was annoying no one else was affected by the cold. I don't know how they all thought twenty degrees was warm. The height of summer, apparently. They wouldn't know what to do with themselves if they ever visited Townsville. Thirty-eight degrees on a good day, though it wasn't the Celsius on the thermometer that was the killer; it was the humidity. Eighty-seven percent if you were lucky, but normally it rose higher. *That* was normal summer weather. This wasn't summer.

Movement attracted my attention, and my breath caught. A silver ghost dog walked through the wall of the classroom. It was exactly the same as the one I saw at the tattoo parlour five days ago. It sat directly in the middle of the front of the room, and I had to sit up straight to see it clearly. It sat like a well-trained cattle dog and appeared to stare at each one of us in turn. I stared at it then carefully glanced around the room. It was studying everyone, taking its time, contemplating. I was pretty sure I was the only one watching it. It was hanging around in the front of the room like it belonged there… and no one was paying it any attention. The lack of surprise in that realisation left a slight sinking feeling. I was the only one who could see it. Again.

The door opened, and a guy in black trousers, a pale blue dress shirt, and a tie decorated with the TARDIS from *Dr Who,* walked in. Not Mr Goss. He had dark receding and the start of a pot belly.

"Good afternoon, class. My name is Mr Borradaile, and I'll be your teacher today. According to…" he consulted a piece of paper, "…Mr Goss, you ought to be continuing your assignment work. You should have also all received and have brought with you a copy of the book… *The Secret River.* Take your books out."

There was a general shuffle of papers, books, and pencil cases as everyone did what he said. I could see from the bookmark in Evie's book she had nearly finished reading the damn book. I didn't use a bookmark or dog ear the page. I didn't need to. I opened the book to page ten. It was as far as I had read. It was a boring book. Instead of reading, I watched the silver ghost dog. It wandered around the room, turning its soul-deep black eyes in the direction of the student who answered to their name as Mr Borradaile did the roll-call.

I licked my lips, a little freaked out. I was pretty sure it could understand and was locking in our faces to our names, searing it into its memory.

"Ginnifer Martin?"

I nearly couldn't answer. If I did, it would know me and I would never be able to escape it.

"Ginnifer Martin?" Mr Borradaile called out again.

"She's here, sir." Evie pointed at me.

The dog turned its gaze and trained those onyx eyes directly on mine, daring me to escape its mental catalogue and taunting me with the knowledge that I couldn't.

"What are you?" I breathed, barely mouthing the words.

It lifted its long, snouted head and slowly blinked at me with those depth-defying black eyes. I hissed my breath in slowly. It did understand.

"Alice Michaels?"

"Here."

It took itself off to Alice's desk but looked back at me along the way. After Mr Borradaile finished the roll-call, it went and sat beside the teacher's desk at the front of the room.

Watching.

Eyes focused, barely blinking.

It was hard enough to read the words in the book as it was, and it didn't help I kept looking up at the dog. It sat there, pulling my attention like a magnet. Forcing myself, I attempted to pay attention to the words on the page, struggling through half a page and fighting the impulse to throw the book across the room. How anyone could want to read this stupid book was beyond me. With a sigh, I turned the page and rubbed my eyes. For what had to be the thousandth time, I wished the words would stay still. I hated reading. It was impossible when the letters never stayed in the same place.

Gradually, I became aware of a warmth

radiating through my feet and up my legs and sighed in relief, before I figured out the heat was strange. The heaters for the room were on the walls near the ceiling, and they weren't on. Moving back a little, I peeked down under my desk and nearly had a heart attack. My white-knuckled grip on the edge of the desk was the only thing stopping me from taking a flying leap backwards into the wall. The dog was there. It dropped itself from sitting to lying through my feet. I held myself stock-still, forcing myself to breathe. It didn't attack or possess me. In fact, it looked like it was taking a nap.

Under my desk.

Through my feet.

I didn't know what it was or what it wanted from me, but I did know one thing. The ghost dog was like a little heater, and I could handle that. I sat back up before I attracted attention and pretended to focus on the book.

Finally, the bell rang to end the torture, and I couldn't close the book fast enough. I jammed it between the pages of my notebook, dumped it on the pile of books I'd needed for my previous hospitality class, and clutched the whole pile to my chest, before dropping my pencil case. Slowly, I reached down for it. The dog was still there, under the table. It moved only its eyes to look at me, and I thought the small move made it seem kind of sad.

"Thank you," I whispered to the dog.

He blinked then yawned. I jerked upright, narrowly missing smacking my head against the desk. As amazing as the warm ghost critter was, its yawn was the stuff of nightmares. Its mouth was huge and its teeth looked damn sharp. Ghost or not, I was pretty sure it could take a sizable bite out of me if it wanted to. Hugging my books to my chest, I squeezed past the chairs and got trapped by the slowly exiting crowd at the door.

"Ginnifer Martin, would you stay for a second?"

Heart sinking, I slowly turned around. Perhaps he had mixed me up with another student. Mr Borradaile was leaning against his desk with his arms crossed looking directly at me. I turned back toward the crowd, which had apparently magically disappeared in seconds flat. I sighed and did what I didn't want to do. I turned back to him and took the three steps that brought me to a polite distance.

"Yes, sir?"

Uncrossing his arms, he went behind the desk. "Take your book out please."

"My book?"

"The one you were supposed to be reading."

I swallowed. "Why?"

"I want to check something."

Looking down at the silver dog who had sat beside me, I slowly unearthed it from between the blank pages of my notebook and held it out.

"Read to me where you're up to."

My stomach filled with dread. It was Townsville all over again. "Why?"

"Humour me."

"I don't think it's very funny."

"Read it, Ginnifer."

I held it out farther, closer to him. "If you want to know the story, you can read it. I don't mind."

"I want to hear you read it."

"Why?"

"Just read it."

My mouth went dry and my hand began to

shake. I wasn't cold any more, but very, very hot. "You know, sir, it is home time. I have to catch a bus."

"This'll take two minutes."

"Why do you want me to read it?"

"Why don't you want to read it?"

"I don't like reading out loud."

He nodded. "I see. Is it because you have dyslexia?"

If he'd hit me, I wouldn't have been more shocked. I stared at him, my eyes narrowing. "How'd you know that?"

"A guess." He tapped the cover of the book in my hand. "This has an audiobook available, you know. I'd consider that if I were you."

Picking up his papers, he ran his hand over his tie and walked out of the room. I could only look down at the silver dog.

"A guess? Really? Dyslexia is rare in girls. I'm pretty sure it's not the first thing people think of."

It didn't respond. Not even a blink. It stared at me for a long moment then sauntered through the wall. I was alone in the room.

Rushing to the door, I watched Mr Borradaile walk the pathway between the buildings, skirting around students. The silver dog didn't skirt. It walked directly through everybody. I followed it until it disappeared then stopped short as a realisation smacked me in the head so hard it nearly hurt. If I didn't have to catch a bus, I would have tried to scope the teacher's car park, because the ghost dog had gone through the wall of the staff room seconds after Mr Borradaile had used the door. This had gone far enough. I was getting to the bottom of this.

Ghost dogs didn't hang around for no reason, and unless I missed my guess, this one was following the far too perceptive Mr Borradaile.

Chapter Three

I wasn't a photographer, but my phone did the job. With my hands on my hips, I stared up at the photographs tacked to the wall.

The Painted Serpent.

The school.

My backyard.

The three places I'd seen the silver ghost dog.

"Ginny," Dad called out from his office, then came down the hallway to my room. He stumbled against my doorframe for a second before he steadied himself. "Whoa."

"Are you okay?" Frowning, I spun in alarm and nearly knocked over my mirror stand that stood directly against the wall in the corner.

"Vertigo. Happens sometimes. Don't worry about it." He held out my sketchbook as I made sure the mirror was steady. "I've scanned your drawings and emailed it to you. I've got to say, this is a brilliant rendition of a Tasmanian tiger. I didn't realise you could draw this well."

"Tasmanian tiger? There are tigers here?"

"Common name for a thylacine. It's a carnivorous marsupial. Extinct now, but some people claim to see them even today. How'd you draw it if you didn't know what it was?"

I shrugged as I took the sketchpad from him. "I saw it at the tattoo place."

"Fair enough. Come on, we're going to be late if we don't leave now."

I sighed. I didn't really want to go. I'd spent the last two and a half weeks trying to figure out the ghosts, with nothing to show for it. With Dad recognising them, I now had a better starting point.

"Ginny, come on."

I could already hear him at the door between the kitchen and garage and shook my head. Shoving the sketchpad into my backpack, I slung it over my shoulder, grabbed a jacket to pull over my hoodie, and followed him out to the car. "Where are we going?"

"It's a surprise."

"I'm not sure I like surprises."

"You'll like this one."

When we got to town, he told me to close my eyes.

"Seriously?" I stared at him.

"Yes. I told you, it's a surprise."

It was official. My dad was a dag.

"Un-freaking-believable."

"Please?"

Blowing out a deep breath, I crossed my arms and did what he wanted. "Fine."

"Thank you. Now don't open them until we get there."

"Like I'll know when that is."

He laughed. "I'll let you know."

I'd never travelled in a car with my eyes closed before, and it wasn't something I'd do again in a hurry. It was disconcerting, and each corner, slow down, and speed up felt like I was getting tossed around. I never realised how much I relied on sight to hold myself upright in the seat. As we travelled, I tried to listen for clues. Not an easy task with the windows wound up and the heater on. By the time Dad slowed to a stop on what sounded a little like gravel, I was completely lost.

"Can I open my eyes now?"

"Yep."

Dad sounded pleased with himself as I opened my eyes. I saw the back of the Mount Lyall Motor Inn. I only recognised that, because large, faded red-and-white letters announced the name of the building, but that's not where Dad took me.

"Where are we?"

"Come on, out of the car."

He led the way across the car park to a grassy area with a white picket fence. The fence made a circle surrounding a good-sized round pit with a single rail line cutting across it. The rail line led into a yellow shed-type building with red trim and high glass windows interconnecting to make an arch. Smack bang in the middle of the windows was a clock.

"A train station?"

"That's not all." Dad placed his hand on my shoulder and guided me through the door of the station. "Check this out."

A green steam train with quaint red wagons sitting on a track on the inside of a glass-roofed station was not what I was expecting. Except that the colours of the station were bright yellow and cheerful pale wood, it could have come out of a movie set at the turn of the century.

"What is this? Platform nine and three-quarters?"

"This is the West Coast Wilderness Railway." He announced it like it was a famous thing.

"Okay?" I shrugged.

"It's like going back in time. You'll love it."

It was obvious he loved it. He was wide-eyed and grinning like a kid at Christmas, but history and all that was not my idea of fun. I shook my head and followed him to the ticket booth. When I saw the price for one ticket, I nearly had a heart attack.

"Dad, you don't have to do this."

"Sure, I do. Besides, Cornelia is expecting us."

"Cornelia? From your work, Cornelia? The one who bakes?"

"Yeah. This was her idea. Show you the best that Tasmania has to offer. I haven't done this in ages, so I jumped at the chance."

"Do you and Cornelia have a... thing?"

"What?" He looked shocked then laughed. "No. I think her husband would have something to say about that. Come on, she should be at the Track Café."

A small café, a building within the station building, sitting like an antiquated room built as an afterthought, wasn't too far from the ticket office. The idea of a building inside a larger building was kind of fun though, and I wondered if the inside would match the outer building Dad pointed through the wide window when we walked past.

"There she is."

I came to a dead halt as Dad continued through the doors, all thoughts of buildings fading away like water seeping through sand.

It was back.

And this time, it had a friend.

Two silver dogs were inside the café. One was sitting near a table, while the other was slowly walking through tables, chairs, and people. Back and forth. Almost like it was casually pacing.

"Ginny?"

I looked up. Dad was standing directly through the sitting silver dog, beckoning me. My whole body screamed at me to run. I even took a step back. Then I saw a little girl, no more than three or four, walk straight through the pacing dog. Nobody was reacting to them. It was just me. I closed my eyes for a second and took a slow breath. I had to treat this like a Drawing image. No one else could see those either.

Hiding my left hand in the pocket of my jacket, I repeatedly flexed and clenched a fist. It was comforting and familiar, even if it didn't diminish the dogs. On wooden, shaky legs, I stepped through the door and approached the table to the left of Dad, keeping well away from both dogs. Although if they were as warm as the one at school, then maybe I was being a little too cautious.

"Ginny, this is Cornelia Borradaile and her son Joshua." He indicated to each of them then to me. "This is Ginny."

"Hi." I gave a small wave.

Cornelia had short, dusty-blonde hair mixed with grey, and my first impression was her friendly face with kind of a cheeky smile. The lines around her amazing blue eyes made me think she was someone who laughed a lot.

Her son looked vaguely familiar, but the black

cap with the blue charging rhino cast a shadow over his face and made it hard to tell. I could tell his hair was long enough to be tied back in a low ponytail at the nape of his neck, and was captivated by the curl of sandy-blond hair behind his ear that wasn't quite long enough to be bound by the hair tie.

"I think we've met." Joshua waved a finger in my direction. "Hang on, you're the girl who asked Barbara for the apprenticeship. You know you left your portfolio behind, right?"

I drew in a sharp breath. No wonder he looked familiar. He was the guy at the Painted Serpent.

Uneasily, I looked down as the pacing silver dog came and plonked itself far too close to me. I watched it for a few seconds, but it played "good dog" and didn't seem to want to take a bite out of me or anything. It didn't yawn either. I wasn't sure I could handle another one of those right now. A hot shiver ran through me as a rushing sound filled my head. I snapped my gaze back to Joshua, blinking until the shadowed darkening of my vision cleared.

The Painted Serpent.

Here.

The silver dog. Thyla... tiger thingy.

Joshua was a possible common thread.

Possibly.

Maybe.

He might be followed by the dog too. If he was, that was two explained. Not the one outside our house, however, and not the second one sitting through Dad's feet.

"Are you okay?"

I blinked. Dad was peering down at me, and the other two were standing. I hadn't moved and was standing in the way like an idiot. "Yeah... I just...

um… can't believe I was stupid enough to lose my portfolio and not realise it."

"It's okay. It's safe and sound. You can pick it up any time," Joshua told me.

"Or Josh can pass it along to me and I can give it to your dad at work. Whichever is easiest." Cornelia briefly patted my shoulder. "All aboard! The train is about to leave."

I had to admit the train carriage was kind of cool. Decorative details matched the historical aspects of both the station and the engine, and it had wide seats and tables in booth formations. I didn't even know trains had tables. Cornelia slid into a booth and the rest of us followed. Including the silver dogs. Trying to act casual, I peered under the table. The dogs got themselves comfortable and curled up through our feet. Instant heat radiated from my feet up my legs. The change in temperature made me shiver, and as freaky as it was to see my feet through a silver ghost dog, the heat was beautiful. The one at school, these tow here…apparently, they all emitted heat. That was cool.

"What are you doing?" On the opposite side of the table, Dad leaned back and peered under as well.

"Nothing… just… they have all this fancy historical stuff everywhere. I was checking if they skimped where no one could see."

"And?" Cornelia sounded amused.

"And…" I peered under again, this time looking at the detail on the carriage. "No skimping."

This time, she laughed. "Glad to hear it."

It was easier to ignore the silver dogs when a table hid them, and so long as I pretended the train carriage was heated, I was fine.

A high-pitched whistle blew followed by the classic speaker-muffled voice giving the final warning and we were off. A blonde woman in a smart navy-blue suit and green scarf with a microphone introduced herself and gave us the housekeeping speech. After that, she launched into tour guide mode, talking about the size of the tracks, the history of the train line, and a whole list of other things I tuned out after a while.

So not my thing.

I was right next to the window and stared out over the rainforest-like landscape. Seriously, ferns and trees practically touched the carriage as it went past. The smoke puffed overhead, and when it got between the hazy, watery sun and us, the air and shadows took on an eerie, slightly sickly sepia hue. It was almost hypnotic watching the shadow of smoke against the landscape.

The train stopped at some small places along the line. Even though I was told the names of them a few times, they didn't sink in. We panned for gold at one of the places, where the cold water and shaded spot had me shivering and seeking out a ghost dog to stand through, and went for a rainforest walk at another. Everything was so green. After living in a town with something like 50 mls of rain in the last ten years, greenery took some getting used to.

Back in the train, I stared out the window, immersed in the landscape, while the others engaged in conversation that washed over me. At times some of the land next to the tracks dropped away to nothing but gullies of tree tops and emptiness enhanced by the pale gold orb of a sun half hidden by oily clouds. Other times we clattered over bridges decades old that looked ready to fall into an abyss. Yet at other times we were encased in forest and greenery so dense I wondered if there would ever be another side.

"Are you okay?"

I jumped a mile at Joshua's voice. "Yeah, why?"

"You keep hitting me with your hand."

Automatically, I clenched my fist. While I had been looking out the window, I hadn't noticed the Drawing image in front of my eyes, but as I turned to look at him, I did. The image was of trees, a landscape similar to what I'd been seeing out the window, washing a pink haze in front of my eyes.

"Yeah, sorry. Trying to suppress the urge to draw."

"So, you have to hit me?" He sounded more amused than upset.

"I wasn't hitting you. Not deliberately. Moving my hand helps."

"Helps what?"

"Suppress the urge."

"What do you want to draw?"

"The scenery."

Dad leaned forward. "What's stopping you?"

My eyebrows shot up. "I'm out and about… you know, with people."

"Kiddo, if you want to draw, draw."

"You won't think it's rude?"

Cornelia lifted her hands in an "I'm not stopping you" pose. "Not me."

"I've seen your drawings, and they're pretty good."

I turned to Joshua. "You have?"

"You did leave your portfolio on the counter."

I gave a nod. He had a point. Opening my bag, I pulled out my sketchpad and pencils before anyone changed their mind. If Mum had been here, she would have absolutely ridden me about drawing when we were out with people. Actually, if Mum were here, I would have had five half-sisters to look after, so I wouldn't have had the chance to draw. It was such a relief to be able to sketch what I saw and have the Drawing image fade away without having to fight it for the rest of the day.

"Whoa."

When I finally looked up, Joshua was staring down at the page and Dad and Cornelia were in another booth across the carriage. Cornelia was showing Dad how to use her camera.

"Whoa... what?" I turned back to Joshua.

"That is amazing. It's so real. I can do cartoons and the like, but this... this is like a black-and-white photo. The detail is brilliant. The depth, the perspective. Why the hell do you want to be a tattoo artist? You could make it big by framing and selling these."

"Yeah, right."

"I'm serious. Can I see the rest of your drawings?"

"Sure." I shrugged, moving the book across the table toward him.

He flipped through a few pages. "Wow. This is amazing. You can't see this person's face, but it's so clear they are upset.

Josh pointed to a drawing of a person—I thought it could be a girl—in a hoodie, sitting against a tree in a wooded area. Her head was bowed over the knee she had pulled up and wrapped her arms around. I'd drawn it months ago, back in

33

Townsville. I'd sat in the girls' bathroom in
Castletown shopping centre to hide the need to get
the Drawing image down on paper.

With my head on my hand, I watched him turn
the pages backward through the book. When he
reached the page with the drawings of the silver
dog, I zeroed in on his reaction.

"These thylacine are… wow, I can't get over
how lifelike they are." He ran his fingers lightly
over the page.

"How do you know what they are?"

He laughed. "I'm Tasmanian. Of course I know
what they are. There's a museum about them and
everything. They're like a national mascot around
here."

I smiled. "Cool."

That wasn't what I wanted him to tell me, but
what did I expect? For him to say *"Sure do. I have a
ghost one that follows me around"*? Like that was
going to happen.

A high-pitched screech tore into my ear drums
and the whole world dropped out from under us. My
head collided with the glass and I was tossed around
like a ragdoll. The whole world itself was writhing
in sickly orange agony.

Then nothing.

Aside from my heart echoing in my head, there
was no sound whatsoever. The carriage was still,
and a huge billow of steam overhead caused the
light to ooze between grainy brown, sickly orange,
and washed-out blue, almost stretching into all three
hues at once. Gradually, sound came back into the
world. Some kid was crying, and a low murmur of
conversation was starting to wash through the
carriage.

"Is everyone okay?" Dad's voice was overwhelmingly loud.

"Ouch." I winced, holding my head.

"Ginny?" Within seconds, Dad and Cornelia were at our booth.

"I'm okay. I smacked the window."

"Move your hand." Cornelia waved Joshua out from beside me and checked my head. "Close your eyes for a sec. Okay, now slowly open them. Are you seeing double?"

"No."

"Yeah, you're okay. You'll probably have a bruise though."

"She's fine?" Dad asked.

"Yeah."

Dad gave her a nod and went off down the carriage, checking on everyone else. The carriage was upright, and when people started to move around, nothing rocked more than normal. I thought we'd at least be tilted at a crazy angle, or something to indicate what the hell had happened.

"You okay?" Cornelia asked Josh.

"Yeah. What happened?"

"I'm not sure. Sudden urge for a lunch break?"

Holding my head, I silently groaned at her joke.

"Ladies and gentlemen, please stay in the carriage." The blonde railway employee held out her hands as if the move would stop people from leaving. "I'll go and check on what happened. I'm sure we're all fine."

"She wanted the lunch," Cornelia whispered.

I gave her the laugh she wanted and she patted my shoulder as Dad returned.

"Mostly shaken up. Looks like you're the only one with an injury, Gin."

"Yeah, I'm special like that."

Around us, the murmur of conversation was gradually getting louder as we waited. Some of the passengers were moving to the windows and doors, trying to see. Not that there was much to see. All I saw were trees and bushes right against the glass of the window. Other than the fact we'd stopped, there was nothing to show what had happened, and I'm pretty sure that was what was concerning people more. In the distance, I could hear the sound of metal on metal occasionally ringing out. It had no pattern or rhythm, but it clanged once or twice, and then a few seconds later once again.

There was a general surge as the carriage door opened, and a guy in a similar uniform to the blonde lady entered. "Ladies and gentlemen, there is no cause for alarm, but we have had a minor derailment."

"Minor? How is a derailment minor?" someone yelled out from the other end of the carriage.

"Minor, as in we have merely slipped the tracks. There appears to have been some debris on the track. There is no damage. Our crew is prepared for things like this and they'll have the train ready to continue in about an hour. I apologise for the delay, but they will be working as fast as they can."

"Can we leave the carriage?" a woman in orange asked.

"Yes. There is a small clearing to the left-hand side of the train. However, I must ask, if you do choose to disembark, you give your name to me and remain in sight of the train at all times."

The murmur of conversation got loud again as the employee left. It faded down a few minutes later when most of the other passengers left the train.

"Do you guys want to go outside?"

"I'm fine here, Dad." I folded my arms on the table and put my head down. "I'm starting to get a headache."

"Here." Cornelia reached into her handbag and pulled out a packet of painkillers.

"Well, I'm going to go watch them re-rail the train." Dad grinned. "I've never seen that before."

Joshua followed him out, trailing a silver thyla… tiger… thingy behind him, leaving the other one and Cornelia with me. I stared down at it. If that one followed Josh, then this one might follow Cornelia. After all, they were related. It was possible. In fact, I liked it as a theory. It would explain things a little more.

"You don't have to keep me company, you know."

"I know." She slid across the seat on the other side of the booth until she sat against the wall with her legs out on the seat. "But it's got to be colder out there in the wind."

"I can't believe it's February. Did someone forget to tell the weatherman it's summer?"

"It gets warm sometimes."

"When?"

"Well, last year it got warm… on a Wednesday afternoon."

I propped my head up on my hand. "You don't like the cold much either?"

"I don't mind it. Means I get to wear all my gorgeous winter jackets all year round."

"That's fine if you have them."

Cornelia laughed. "We'll have to get you some. I don't mind the excuse for a shopping trip."

That was a little too buddy-buddy for my

comfort, and I chose not to comment.

"So, what's the deal with you and my Dad? I know you're married."

"Your dad and I are friends. He plays darts with Monty."

"Monty?"

"Montgomery. My husband."

"Cornelia and Montgomery. Did you two pop out of the eighteenth century or something?"

She laughed. "No, but as it happens, we were both named after grandparents."

"Oh goody."

"Yours isn't too modern either. Short for Ginevra, I'm guessing?"

I made the sound like a "wrong-answer" buzzer. "Ginnifer. My dad was the one who went to the register, and it turns out… he can't spell Jennifer."

Cornelia grinned and shook her head. "Spelling is definitely not his strong suit. Reading and computers he doesn't like much, but put him in the field and there is no better Ranger around. He's lucky I don't mind paperwork."

The carriage rocked a little as Joshua came back in.

"Hey, Ginny. You should check this out."

Josh stood near the booth with his hands in the pockets of his jacket, but his silver tiger thingy was racing around the carriage like a puppy on red cordial.

"What?"

"Just a cool landscape." He reached across and picked up my sketchbook. "Come on."

Shaking my head, I grabbed my case of pencils and followed him out. I was glad Cornelia's painkillers were kicking in. He led the way along the train to the front of the engine then stepped off into the bush to the right and kept going.

"We're not supposed to lose sight of the train," I reminded him as his silver thyla-thing disappeared into the trees.

"We're not." A few steps further, he turned around. "Here."

I glanced around. Trees, ferns, and other plants. There wasn't even an interesting rocky outcrop or anything. "And?"

Closing the two steps between us, he grabbed my shoulders and spun me around. "Right there."

Through the trees, I could see the front end of the train and vegetation. "Why would I want to draw this?"

"I don't know." He opened my sketchbook and held it up to me. "You tell me."

"I don't—"

"Look at the sketch, Ginny. The one you drew on the train."

I felt a tightening in my chest as I looked, and tried to play it cool. "And?"

"Oh, for Pete's sake. Look at the sketch. Imagine there's a train in the picture. Then look at what's in front of you."

"Intense much," I told him as I took the book. I had the feeling I wouldn't need the confirmation, but I did what he wanted. I looked at the sketch, and then the scene in front of me. I nearly couldn't swallow. This couldn't be happening. The drawing was missing the train in the background, but otherwise the two scenes were identical, and Josh sounded like he'd figured it out. My stomach dropped down to my boots, and I struggled to think of the correct response.

"What the hell?"

"My point exactly." He pointed down at the page. "Now look at the sketch again. Right here."

It was difficult to breathe as I looked down at his pointer finger and back to the real scene. The train had derailed right at the point of—

"Ginny, why did you draw pebbles on the train tracks here? Right here?"

Giving a shrug, I made a singsong hum to indicate I had no idea while praying he hadn't worked out what my Drawing images meant.

He grabbed my hand and pulled me closer to the train, pointing to where two crew members were working. "See that little pile of pebbles there? I watched them pull those out from the tracks. From under the train."

A shiver ran down my spine, but I shook it off. He was clutching at straws. He had to be. There was no way he'd figured it out. It wasn't possible. "Wow, what a cool coincidence. Don't you think?"

"No, I don't think. I think you drew the future."

Oh shit.

I stared at him then burst out laughing, hoping it didn't sound forced. "You're crazy. It's just a drawing."

"A drawing that predicted there would be pebbles on the track."

"Ah, but not a train derailment. Little flaw in your theory, mate."

"Ginny…" He trailed off then removed his hat to push his hair back, dislodging a few strands from the hair tie in the process.

"What?"

"Does anyone else in your family have violet

40

eyes?"

I blinked, gripped with dread by his change of topic. "Blue eyes. And yes, my mum does."

"The same colour blue?"

"Well, no. Mine are darker."

"And they went violet when you were drawing."

I didn't know what to say. It took a few heart-pounding seconds to shove my brain into gear. Seconds, I'm sure he noticed. "If they did, it was an optical illusion caused by some lights. An optometrist told me that."

"He was wrong."

"She. And what does it matter, anyway? It's only eye colour."

"Eye colour that changes from dark blue to violet when you were drawing an image of the future. Yep. Doesn't matter at all."

"Oh, come off it." I laughed. "You think because I went through a patch of funny light when I drew this picture it's predicting the future? Would you listen to yourself?"

Joshua replaced his cap then slowly hooked his thumbs into the pocket of his trousers. "It does sound a little crazy."

"A little? Slight understatement, don't you think?"

"Perhaps." He took a breath like he was going to say something else, but obviously, he changed his mind, because he simply turned and walked away instead.

I'd had the Drawing images for as long as I could remember, and Mum said I'd started drawing the second I picked up a pencil, but no one—not family, not friends—knew I could draw the future.

Even the shrink didn't believe me. Within an hour of knowing me, Josh had picked it. That had never happened before. Ever. What the hell was I supposed to do now?

Chapter Four

It was three o'clock by the time we got home, and the pale sun was already drained of most of its strength, nearly giving way to the clouds as though it couldn't keep shining long enough to hold on until dusk. The train trip was only supposed to be a half day outing, but the derailment had put us behind and Dad was eager to get some work done in the garage. I made a cuppa for both of us and disappeared into my room, smelling the semi-sweet burn with the acrid aftertaste that was fast becoming familiar. The first time I'd smelled what turned out to be Dad soldering lead, I'd panicked, thinking I'd accidentally left something burning. Now it was almost a background thing, a part of life in this house. Almost.

In my room, I pulled out my sketchbook. Josh's words rang clear in my mind as I ran my fingers lightly over the drawing of pebbles on the track. Because I drew all the time and deliberately had three or four books on the go, no one knew when I'd done the drawings, and I'd learned not to date them.

Most of the time, they assumed I'd done the drawings after the event. Today was the first time someone had figured it out. It wasn't the first time anyone knew about it. But last time, they didn't figure it out. I told them, and I got sent to a shrink and made to take medication for my efforts. I had to stay away from Josh. That was all there was to it. Hopefully, he'd forget all about it or convince himself he'd imagined it, or something.

Leaving my room, I went out to the garage and leaned against the doorframe between the kitchen and the garage. "Hey, Dad?"

"Yeah?" He looked up from soldering his stained-glass art piece.

"How often do you see Josh?"

He shrugged. "Not much."

"He doesn't go to school, does he?"

"Graduated about two years ago, I think. Why?"

"Just wondering. Didn't think I'd seen him there. Or much around the place."

"Well, that would be true, considering you don't do anything out of the house except school."

I pushed off the doorframe. "We live nearly ten kilometres out of town, Dad, and all I have is a push bike. It's a little hard."

"At least you have the bike."

"True. But when I get a job, the first thing I'm going to buy is a car."

"That's totally up to you."

Back home, Mum only had one car, but she let me drive it when I needed to. Of course, Dad only had one, but I wasn't listed on his insurance yet. I knew they weren't the cheapest things going, but it sucked not having transport. I had my licence, I just didn't have a car.

"Did you get the speech-to-text software working?" Dad asked as I turned to walk away.

"Kind of. I have to get used to the whole 'comma' and 'next paragraph' deal."

"You'll get used to it. I did. Pretty soon, it'll be second nature."

I gave a quick noncommittal grin and left him to his glass making. I'd never come across anyone who did stained glass things before, but he was pretty good at it. He had some cool designs, including a plane with a glass propeller that could spin. He sold them in a shop in town, plus a couple of markets a month when he wasn't working. At least I knew where my artistic streak came from, which was nice. Nobody else at home could draw. It sucked that I now also knew where my dyslexia came from, too.

Back in my room, I sat at my homework desk and unearthed my MP3 player. At least Mr Borradaile had been good for something. The audiobook idea was brilliant. It didn't make the stupid book any less boring, but I was on my fourth read-through. I couldn't believe, for the first time in years, I had an English assignment nearly finished on time. I felt pretty smart for a change.

My hand hovered over the Play button for a second before I froze. Lowering my hand, I sat upright in the chair.

Mr Borradaile.

He had the same last name as Josh and Cornelia.

And he also had a silver ghostly thylacine.

Grabbing a Post-it, I wrote their last name as best I could, since I didn't actually know how to spell it, and stuck it to the wall beside my wardrobe, under the photos. This had to be the link. The tattoo parlour, the school, the train. Each time, a Borradaile had been around. The only time it hadn't been true was the thylacine in the backyard. Staring at the photos for a few seconds, I tapped the one of the backyard before leaving my room. Outside was colder than it had been earlier, but I didn't go back for my jacket. I zipped the hoodie as I walked to the spot where I'd seen the thylacine that night. I'd already checked it out when I took the photo, but this time I had a different question. If the Borradailes were the link, then someone in that family had to have been out here that night. The spot was along the turning circle near the driveway, barely within the wash of the outside light.

"Just because you were here, doesn't mean a Borradaile was this close. I don't know how far away from them you can travel." I spoke to the memory of the thylacine. "I don't remember hearing a car that night. So what? They parked on the highway and walked in? The driveway is over a kilometre long. They would have had to be keen."

Shoving my hands into the pockets of my jumper, I moved further away from the driveway, into the bush that surrounded the house. It was a good fifteen to twenty meters from the driveway. If someone had been standing anywhere in the tree line wearing dark clothing, it was possible I wouldn't have seen them. I was focused on the thylacine, after all. The only thing was, I had no evidence. It had rained between then and now. In fact, yesterday's downpour could have washed all evidence from a crime scene, let alone a few possible marks in this area. I had nothing.

Turning to look into the bush, I thought I saw something. Carefully, I took a few steps forward and peered around the nearest gum tree. There was only a few thin bushes and scraggly trees between me and the thylacine. I was pretty sure if it could see me, it would somehow relay that back to the Borradaile behind it. As quietly as I could, I moved further around. It stayed standing there. With a quick breath, I boldly walked up to the thylacine. After all, I had all the right in the world to be in my own backyard. It pulled itself to its feet as I stepped into it, feeling the heat from its ghostly body. If the Borradaile could receive information through the ghost, they would know I was there. It was their move next.

The thylacine took a few steps back into the bush and I followed it. As it backtracked through the greenery, I followed it step for step. Almost. I had to go around the trees it went through. Standing in a small area free of trees, it stopped walking for a second and watched me.

"Yeah," I told it. "I ain't giving up."

Directly in front of me, I heard a twig snap before the thylacine took off running in the same direction. I bolted after it, dodging trees and bushes, skidding through undergrowth and mud, and jumping over fallen logs. This was not a good way to keep up with a silver ghost that could run directly through obstacles. It wasn't long before I stood, bent over, with my hands on my thighs, gasping for oxygen. My throat and chest burned with the cold air. I took deep, gasping breaths, waiting for the thylacine to move. Its head was turned in my direction, but its body was angled away as though prepared for flight. If it took off again, I was ready.

As soon as I could breathe. Hearing the rustle of foliage, I spun around and came face-to-face with Joshua, who skidded to a stop.

"It was you. I knew it," I panted. "What the hell are you doing spying on my house?"

He was breathing heavily, but he wasn't gasping for air like I was. "I wasn't spying."

"Bullshit, you weren't."

"I came to drop off your portfolio."

I stared pointedly at his empty hands. "Sure, you were. And you were running through the bush, because…?"

"I got to your house and saw you take off. I thought something might be wrong."

"And you came by hovercraft? Because I sure as hell didn't hear an engine."

"I walked."

Noticing the hesitation before his words, I stood, shoving my hands on my hips, still trying to drag air into my lungs. I was so damn unfit. Josh stood there, his breathing back to normal already. "Pull the other one, it plays 'Jingle Bells.'"

"I did. I live a few kilometres that way." He pointed. "Just over that ridge."

"Where's the portfolio, hey?"

He took a step closer and I took a step back. "Look, I'm not going to hurt you, okay?"

"You didn't answer the question."

"All right. Fine. I don't have it."

"So, you were spying?"

"I wasn't —"

"Don't come any closer."

I pointed at him as he took a few steps. His hands went up as though surrendering, and he stopped. I still moved further back to keep the same distance between us.

"It's not what you think."

"Oh yeah? So tell me, Joshua, why do you randomly walk a 'few kilometres'…" I made air quotation marks. "…to stand at our driveway? Got a thing for the architecture of our house, do you?"

"I wasn't standing at your driveway."

"Close enough."

"How the hell did you know I was there, anyway? I wasn't close enough to see your house. There's no way you could have seen me."

"You'd be amazed at what I can see."

"Yeah, like the future."

I crossed my arms and took another step back. "You're avoiding answering the question. Don't think I haven't noticed."

"Okay, fine. You got me. Yes, I came over to talk to you. I hadn't figured out how or what to say, so I was standing there trying to psych myself into it. Is that a crime?"

"What about a month ago?"

"What?"

"Nearly a month ago, you stood outside our house at night, watching us. The same day I came to the Painted Serpent. Were you trying to psych yourself up then, too?"

Josh scratched the back of his head, staring up at the tree tops for a moment. "I'd seen your portfolio. I was curious to find out more about you. But it was more to do with the way you reacted at the Painted Serpent."

"How I reacted?"

"You weren't looking at me. You were looking at something else in the room and it terrified you."

I took another step back and there was nothing

under my foot. Time froze for a second, long enough for me to realise I wasn't able to regain my balance, before it snapped back at the same speed my chin smacked the ground. I tumbled and slid down wet, sticky mud mixed with decaying leaves. Grey sky, spinning branches, freezing mud. Rocks bit into my body from every direction and cold, slimy mud covered the world.

Slamming into a tree, feet first, brought me to a horrendous stop, but it didn't last long. Reaching out, I grabbed onto the trunk as the mud threatened to take me further. I could barely hold on. Agony ripped from my ankle up my leg as my fingers slipped over rough bark. I choked on mud and struggled to breathe as the swirling earth tried to drown me. Just as I couldn't hang on any longer, it all stopped. My frantic gasps for air were all I could hear until some bird scared the life out of me by screeching nearby. The noise made me jerk and pain tore up my leg, nearly making me vomit.

I couldn't move. I was so cold and in so much pain. My leg was on fire and nausea nearly overwhelmed me. I lay there, shaking, breathing in the clinging scent of muddy earth. I was so cold. I needed to get warm. With slow movements and the fire of agony clawing at my body, inch by inch, I sat up against the tree and pulled my leg closer to my body. I'd never broken a bone before, but I was pretty sure this was what a broken one felt like. Pain lanced through me like a hot knife twisting through every inch of my leg, stealing even the ability to breathe. My whole body was shaking. I could only grit my teeth and hope not to pass out. I didn't know how far I'd fallen, how far away Josh was, or even if he would be able to hear me if I could call out.

Struggling to wipe the mud off my hand the best I could, I reached for my phone and pulled it out of my pocket.

"No, please no."

The screen was shattered and it had turned itself off. My hands were shaking so much I could barely hold it, let alone succeed in turning it on. It was useless. The damn thing was dead.

"Shit, shit, shit."

A rushing filled my head and I struggled to keep my balance, even against the tree, as my vision blurred and blackened. It eased then came again, and I held my breath until it passed. There wasn't any pain in my head, but something was very wrong. Leaning back against the tree, I hugged the phone to me and stared at the treetops above. I was in my own backyard, and I could possibly die out here.

"Stop being so dramatic." My teeth were chattering so badly I could barely get the words out. "Josh has gone to get Dad. It'll be okay. It'll be okay."

I didn't know if I was shaking with pain or shivering with cold. It was all too much. I pulled my hoodie over my head, wrapped my arms around the knee of my good leg, and burst into tears. I was exhausted by the time the sobbing stopped. The shadows barely moved under the overcast sky, but they were getting darker. It was getting colder. Dried mud made my skin itch. The only positive was as long as I didn't attempt to move, the pain burned but it had stopped making me feel sick. At least I had that.

A rustle came from my left and my head snapped to that direction. The trees were casting misty shadows against the trunks of their neighbours and it was hard to see anything moving. Without warning, a dark shape appeared out of the shadows as if melting into existence. Dark brown fur with near black stripes.

A thylacine.

A real one.

I blinked. Even though the creature was barely metres away, it was blurry. Like someone had taken a picture of it when it moved. It was watching me. Stopping still for a second, the entire world held its breath, and then with a growl, it came at me. Screaming, I lifted my hands to shield my face, expecting to be ripped to pieces, but no attack came. Slowly, I lowered my arms and opened my eyes. The thylacine was sniffing me, its head so close I could feel the heat of its breath. It was hard to make out any features, even this close. Or maybe because it was this close.

Not quite sure if it was real, I reached out and touched its chest. Its fur was short and surprisingly soft, and it even smelled a little like warm dog. It moved its head down and nudged my shoulder this time. Movement behind the thylacine caught my eye, and I curled my fingers in its fur as I looked across.

Joshua.

Naked.

And silver.

I blinked, trying to make sense of what I saw. It was like the two had switched places. Josh was ghostly and silver, and the thylacine was real. Blurry, but real.

Frowning, I looked back at the thylacine.

"Joshua?"

The silver image wavered, like heat waves on a bitumen road in summer, and the silver Joshua shimmered, changing into the thylacine. And it wasn't all that changed. Abruptly, I snatched my hand away from Joshua's naked chest.

"Ginny, are you okay?"

"You… ju… ju —"

"I'll explain everything later, but are you okay? Can you stand up?"

"I…" Joshua's chest was naked, and so were his legs. He was crouched down so I couldn't see anything else, but if his silver image was anything to go by, then… "You're naked."

"Yeah, I can't help it, but are you okay? Can you stand up?"

"I think I broke my ankle." I stared at him.

He looked down at my leg then, still crouched, he moved around behind the tree.

"Where are you going?"

"It's okay. I'm here. I'm checking the slope."

I heard movement behind me. First, it faded, like he'd gone away, but then the sound of movement returned.

"There's no way I can carry you up there. I'm going to get your dad. Hang in there."

He moved off again somewhere behind me. The silver thylacine stood next to me for a few moments then turned and disappeared in the same direction Joshua had gone.

I was alone again. Birds called to each other in the bush, and a chorus of insects started up. A mosquito buzzed around my head until I smacked it against my arm, where it lay as a black mark and red smear on my once green sleeve. Right now, it was easy to believe I was the last human on earth.

Maybe I'd hit my head too, because I had to have imagined that. That whole event wasn't possible. I watched a yellow leaf fall in a graceful sweeping dance from the treetops above and land on the ground beside me. Reaching across, I picked it up. My hand stilled as I held it in my palm and hovered a single grubby finger over the paw print indented in the soft mud. It was the pain. I had to be going mad.

Because there was no possible way Joshua could have appeared from a thylacine.

Chapter Five

"How are you holding up, honey?"

I looked up as Dad came into the hospital cubicle holding the steaming cup of something resembling coffee but looked as black and thick as motor oil. On second thought, "cubicle" was too fancy to describe the space enclosed with a blue curtain in the emergency room. "I'm okay. When can I leave?"

I'd already been wheeled in and out three times for x-rays, some sort of scan in a round tube with loud clunking noises, and another scan that involved getting injected in the leg with something green first.

"The nurse at the desk out there said they were waiting for the doctor to do his rounds. He'll let us know then."

"That's the best news I've heard all day."

"Oh yeah, so what other news have you heard?"

"Not much. Grey flecked floors and cream walls don't say much."

The pain medication they had me on made me

feel nauseated, but at least the pain was bearable. Apparently, I hadn't broken the bone. Just the next best thing. I'd torn the lateral ligament. From the swelling and bruising, I'd say I'd done a pretty decent job of it too. At least it had been swollen and bruised before they'd jammed it into a cast. I think the guy they employed to make up the cast was a dungeon torture boss in his previous life. He had wrenched my foot around like it belonged to an unfeeling mannequin. I was sure he enjoyed my screams of agony.

Movement came from near the doorway, and a silver thylacine slunk through the drawn curtain. I waited. The thylacine sat near the chair next to the grey bedside table, but no one else came into the room.

"Is there someone out there?"

"Probably, it is a hospital. Why?"

"Um… I can see a shadow hovering… kinda."

Dad went across and checked. "Joshua. Don't stand there. Come in."

"I didn't want to intrude."

Joshua's voice from the hallway sent a jolt through me, and in my head I could see him, silver and slightly transparent. I shut my eyes for a second. The paw print had been real.

"Don't be silly. You're not intruding."

Joshua followed Dad back into the enclosed space. His hands were in the pockets of his jacket and his shoulders were slightly hunched. He didn't look very comfortable.

"If it wasn't for you, Ginny could have been stuck at the bottom of that landslide for hours." Dad squeezed Joshua's shoulder for a second. "I'm glad you were driving past when you did."

I played with the corner of the white hospital blanket, wondering what story Joshua told Dad when he reached the house. I was willing to bet it didn't include a thylacine.

I played dumb. "You were driving past?"

"Yeah. Returning your portfolio. I saw you slip."

"When he stopped to check, he couldn't see you and you didn't respond to his calling, so he came to the house and told me."

Looks like I would have won that bet. "I suppose I should thank you."

He shrugged. "It's okay. Anyone would have done it."

Obviously, Joshua didn't want to talk about it with Dad in the room, but this beating-around-the-bush conversation was pissing me off.

"Dad, can you check on when the doc is supposed to do his rounds?"

Dad glanced at me then at Josh. "Sure."

I waited until his footsteps had faded before I spoke in a low voice. "Okay, spill."

"Spill what?"

"Are you really going to play dumb with me, Mr 'I saw you transform naked from a thylacine'?" I hissed at him.

Joshua's hands came out of his jacket fast as he came close to the bed and shushed me. His voice was barely above a whisper. "I was kinda hoping you'd think it was your imagination or something."

So, it was real. "Not a chance."

"Okay. But I can't here. There are too many people who could walk in. But I have to ask you one thing."

"You want me to promise not to tell anyone?

How crazy do you think I want people to know I am?"

"Well, that too, but…" He heaved a sigh, then moved half a step back from the bed. "Oh, God, I hope I'm right about this or Mum's going to kill me for revealing myself to you."

"I can see how getting arrested for indecent exposure would worry you."

"Not that kind of… okay, not *only* that kind, but that's not the point. Just listen, before your dad comes back. When you look at me… my family, is there… something else?"

"Something else?"

"I can't explain it, because I don't have that ability. I'm not…. If I'm right about you, then you should see… something."

"A translucent silver thylacine, perhaps?"

His eyes closed and he sighed. "Thank you. You do see. Thank God."

"You don't see that?"

"No."

"Then what do you see?"

"Nothing."

"Really?"

"Really."

I crossed my arms. "So, what made you think I could see the ghostly thylacine?"

"Your reaction at the Painted Serpent… and the fact you draw the future."

"You're crazy. People do not draw the future."

Joshua laughed. "You do. It's part of what a Seer does."

"A what, now?"

"A Seer."

Joshua took a bigger step away from the bed as

Dad drew back the curtain.

"Hey, Ginny, look who I found wandering the halls."

The doctor and one of the nurses followed him into the room. Frustratingly, Joshua decided now was a good time to skedaddle and took off without giving me his number or any other indication he was going to come good on his promise to tell me what the hell was going on. It was only a matter of time, though. If all else failed, Dad worked with Joshua's mum. If push came to shove, I'd bloody well dob him in to his mum. I'd love to see him try to back-pedal out of it then.

Chapter Six

Feeling as though I was swimming through mud, I pulled myself awake, gasping for breath. My left hand was cramping so badly I could swear it was being crushed. The right side of the top knuckle to my middle finger had been rubbed raw, and I could barely uncurl my hand from around the pencil. Gritting my teeth, I eased my hand flat with the other hand and gingerly began massaging the muscles to ease the pain. Cradling my hand, I lifted my head off my desk. My face felt strange until I peeled away the Post-it note stuck to my cheek. Graphite smudges covered my skin on both hands, and new drawings covered the pages of the sketchbook that had been under my head. It had been years since I'd drawn in my sleep. The first time had been my stepfather, and each time after had shown someone who'd died, or would die.

Flicking on the lamp, I pulled the book closer and studied the drawing. I was looking down at a lap where the head of a dog rested. It was drawn from over the shoulder of the lap owner, a woman, and the dog was simply a dog. Not a silver thylacine, but an honest to goodness dog. This one didn't look too bad. At least there were no visible dead bodies in it. I couldn't tell what was going on though. Perhaps the dog was resting, maybe it was unconscious, or, more likely, as it was the object of the sleep drawing, it was dead. As for who the woman was, or what she was doing, I had no idea.

I turned the page backwards. Most of this page was blacked out with shading. Images were drawn within a large triangle shape, which might have been the light of a torch illuminating a pile of books. It was more of an impression from shapes rather than detailed images, as if the image represented the torchlight moving quickly across a room or wherever. The only hint of what it all could be was a blurred possibility of letters.

C H R O N

It could mean anything. Or nothing. The letters might not even be related to what was supposed to be written. It could all be the muddled up stupid way my mind read words.

The next image made me draw my breath in on a hiss. It was a face. That part was barely recognisable, but it was there. It was barely human. Pitted and weeping lumps, raw and puss-filled lesions twisted and smeared the features. The left side of the mouth corkscrewed up into the nose and whirl-pooled the cheek so the eye was pulled down into an upturned slit. I'd once had to watch a documentary about Joseph Merrick in Social Studies, and the woman in this drawing gave him a run for his money. I think it was a woman; it had long hair.

I turned to the final new image.

A woman lay twisted behind a menacing mouth of gnarled and knotted branches, hiding her face partially from view. I could see her eyes. They were wide open and her stare was vacant. Her stomach was shredded open as glistening entrails spilled out over her hands. I couldn't tell if she was stuck in a tree or if the branches had been used to hide her. My hand went to my mouth. I couldn't believe I'd drawn something so gruesome. The detail was so clear I could almost hear the sticky slide of her guts and smell the hot blood from the page. I swallowed. My throat was gritty and dry, but I didn't taste the bile I was sure I would. I was glad it had been my subconscious mind, or whatever drove the sleep drawings, and I didn't have a memory of seeing the image in my mind first. It was nightmarishly grisly. I could only hope she wasn't still alive when this happened to her.

This was one nightmare I couldn't wake from. Seeing a glimpse of the future and not knowing what to do about it. That was what I hated about these Drawing images. They showed a snapshot of the future, but I never knew what came before or after. I had no context. There was no way of understanding the images. Sometimes, I found out from other people. Like Josh and the train. I would never have guessed the bush scene showed the site of the derailment. Or the drawing showed my stepfather dead, not asleep. There were some drawings I could only guess had come to pass, because I'd drawn years ago, and I don't recall ever seeing them come true. But then they might not have been yet, or maybe they came true for someone else. Or maybe because I'd drawn them and knew they were to happen, they somehow didn't happen, because I'd changed the future by knowing about it. Predicting the future was a tangled knot of string when I started to think about it. Usually, I didn't. Usually, I treated the drawings like drawings until I knew for certain they weren't.

Unwilling to continue looking at the pages, I flipped the book shut and snapped off the light. Between my leg and my hand, it took an age for me to hop-shuffle on one crutch back to bed. Pain throbbed through both my injured limbs, but it was too much effort to go to the bathroom for painkillers. Sleep didn't come. I'd never drawn anything like this before. It could have come from a horror movie. Maybe it was. Maybe it would be a scene I'd catch on some late-night horror festival. It was a feeble attempt at denial and I knew it. I hoped like hell this final image would never happen.

Chapter Seven

"I'm sorry. You want to what?"

I hadn't seen or heard from Josh for a full two and a half days, then he'd sprung this on me.

Josh didn't speak for a moment, but I heard a door close through his end of the phone. I scooted the chair across the gap between my desk and my bed, and bum-hopped across so I could lie down on the bed with my leg on the chair. I was pretty sure I'd heard him wrong. I was *hoping* I'd heard him wrong.

"It wouldn't be a real date or anything. I need a time and place to talk to you without any of your family or mine being around, and this way no one will get suspicious if we disappear together for a few hours."

"And in the middle of our sixty acres wasn't *alone* enough for you?"

"Less chance of a landslide this way."

He had a point.

"Why would it matter if your family was around or not? They've got this whole thylacine thing going for them, too."

I heard him sigh. "I'm not supposed to tell anyone. They would freak if they knew about this."

I'd never gone behind the backs of anybody's parents before. It didn't feel right.

"And if you told them I can see the thylacines?"

"That wouldn't matter to them unless you fit the other indicators."

"What other indicators?"

"That's what I want to talk to you about. But safe to say, you tick two of them. I want to find out the rest."

"And tell me what the hell is with you and your family."

"That too."

I waved my fingers in the air, watching the sun bounce off my skin as it came through my open window. For the first time in days, the sun had come out from behind the clouds, and the sunbeams on my bed were warm. I sighed. I guess it all came down to how much I wanted to find out what was going on.

"Fine. I have no idea what Dad's thoughts are on dating, but if you can come up with a plausible date idea with pick-up and drop-off times, I think he should be fine. I'll ask him when he gets home."

Josh huffed a laugh on the other end of the phone. "There isn't much choice around here, but I'll text you back with details. This Saturday fine with you?"

"So far."

When Josh hung up, I reached up above my head and dropped the phone on the bed, wherever my reach made it land. It was an old Nokia brick Dad had unearthed from somewhere, and it basically only had phone and text functions, which sucked, but it was better than no phone at all. Sitting up, I rolled onto my stomach and scrambled up the bed to where my laptop was sitting on the pillows. Getting myself comfortable in the pillows, I placed the computer on my lap and opened the Thylacine file on my computer. I had a few YouTube videos and documentaries I'd watched, and a handful of articles I'd had my computer read to me. I was starting to hate the computerised, monotone American voice of the program, but it was a hell of a lot better than me trying to read it myself. Basically, in barely over a hundred years after Europeans landed in Tasmania, the thylacine was declared extinct by international standards— whatever they were—and the biggest reason was the bounty for a dead thylacine originally introduced in the eighteen-thirties. A pound a head was probably big money back then, so no wonder it wiped them out. I did try to find out if the Tasmanian population took a hit at the same time. I mean, if thylacines were people like Josh, then it would make sense.

It was too hard to tell. The colonising population was in the thousands, and death rates were high, too. Infant mortality and poor conditions killed people left, right, and centre, as well as a whole heap of stuff I'd never heard of, let alone knew how to pronounce. Diphtheria, typhoid, influenza. I knew measles, but not the rest of it. If the population was dropping at the same rate as the thylacine numbers, there was no way to find out.

"Ginny." Dad's voice came seconds before the sound of the door between the garage and kitchen closing. "You home?"

"Yeah." Standing, I grabbed my crutches. It

would be better if I got this over with. "Hey, Dad?"

He'd kicked off his shoes and was stripping the pale green Rangers uniform shirt off, revealing the black T-shirt underneath. "What?"

"What are your thoughts on dates?"

"Fruit, calendar, or couple?"

"Couple. Josh asked me out this Saturday. I told him I'd have to ask you first, and you'd probably want the where and when. He's going to text me back with details."

"Wow." He disappeared into his room for a second.

"Wow... what?" I called after him.

He returned without his shirt or shoes, pulling the T-shirt free from the waistband of his trousers and leaving it untucked. "I didn't expect you to be so responsible about it."

"I'm full of surprises."

"The more important question is, what do you feel about it? Going out with Josh?"

I shrugged. "He's nice enough, I suppose. He's practically the only person I know outside of school, and aside from school, home, and three seconds around town begging for work, I haven't gone anywhere much."

"What about the Wilderness Railway?"

I rolled my eyes. "You know what I mean."

"I'm happy if you get me the where and when." Opening the fridge, he peered into its depths. "Did you take the steaks out of the freezer this morning?"

"Third shelf."

"I do have one question though."

"What?"

"You've been here three and a half months. You haven't stolen my car, hung out with gang members, or robbed a bank. What the heck did you do to get yourself suspended last year?"

"Mum didn't tell you?"

"Not in so many words. Trouble with schoolwork or something. It didn't really make sense."

"You don't know Mrs Backhash."

"True."

Using my crutches, I swung onto the stool at the kitchen counter. "She asked me to read out loud in English class. I refused."

"And that got you suspended?"

"After about the eighth time, yeah."

"Did anyone tell her you're dyslexic?"

"I don't need everyone at school knowing I'm stupid."

"Having dyslexia doesn't mean you're stupid. It means you ingest information differently."

"Yeah, well, I think they got the idea after Mum ripped Mrs Backhash's head off in a meeting with the principal, but that was after they suspended me."

"And the second time?"

"I asked her a question in class, and she told me to Google the answer. I thought she was supposed to be there to teach, but since she was obviously only in the classroom so she could collect her pay packet, I figured, if she didn't want to teach, then I didn't have to learn. So, I brought comics with me to the rest of her classes, sat in the back, and read them."

"Seriously?"

"Yeah. I can read comics. The words are only in small chunks."

Dad laughed and shook his head. "I can see how that might not have been appreciated."

"Mum didn't think it was that funny."

"I'll bet. I understand now why she needed a new school for you."

"There are other schools back home, you know."

"Ah, yes. But Townsville doesn't have Josh."

In my mind, I saw him as the silver ghost, while his thylacine stood real in front of me. "You have no idea how true that is."

Chapter Eight

The restaurant certainly wasn't five star by any stretch of the imagination. Not that I was expecting five stars. I simply wasn't expecting a plain blue building with a cramped alcove at the entrance with a covered area jutting out, almost like an afterthought, poking its nose into the rough car park. Something about cutting and spite came to mind for some reason. It didn't look promising. It was a good thing I was after information and not necessarily the meal.

Josh held the door and my crutches as I slid out of the car. He hadn't said much during the drive, and he was silent on the walk across the car park. The restaurant might not look like much, but it was apparently pretty popular. There were several other cars we had to weave through, and I caught sight of another couple cutting across the car park too.

"Another family member?"

"What?" Josh seemed surprised I'd spoken.

I gave a nod in the direction of the other couple. "Those two there. Are they related to you?"

Josh shrugged and shook his head. "No. Why?"

"One of them has a thylacine."

"Interesting. I don't know her. But who knows? We could share the same great-uncle or something." He turned back for a second look at the couple then stopped. "This might not be such a good idea."

"You're not backing out now."

"I mean the restaurant. I thought a public place would be okay, but now I'm not so sure. Not if there are other therianthropes here. They could tell the council."

"Theri… what now?"

"What we are."

"So, you're not human?"

"We're human, just…."

"With the ability to change into thylacine."

"Kinda. Yeah."

"Okay, so where do you want to go?"

He thought about it for a second. "You do fast food?"

"On these crutches?" I joked.

His head lowered as he looked at me, and I grinned.

"Yeah, I do fast food."

We went through the drive-through for our burgers, and he took us to the top of the lookout. As he parked, I gazed out over the expanse of town lights reflecting as a hazy glow against the shadow of mountains in the far distance. Tasmania might have a weak imitation of the Townsville sun, hidden behind cloudy skies eight days out of ten, and a serious aversion to the concept of warmth in its weather, but the views were amazing. There was something in the air that made everything so clean and clear. Like a new painting appearing magical with the glisten of wet paint.

"Does your thylacine eat?" I peered into the back seat at it.

Josh did a strange nod-shake of his head then waved a finger at himself. "Not while I'm…."

"Human?"

"Mm-hm." He bit into his burger.

I started to eat mine while I waited for him to start talking. I finished the burger, chips, and was nearly through my thick-shake before that happened.

"This is hard," he told me. "Those who know, know, and those who don't, we don't tell."

"How do those who know learn about it?"

"They're therianthropes. They can feel the beast."

"What exactly is a theri-what's it?"

"It comes from 'Therion' meaning 'beast' and 'Anthropos' meaning 'human being.' Specifically, in relation to shifting between the two."

"Like a werewolf?"

He hummed a half negative, half positive sound. "Same concept, but not ruled by the moonlight."

"Cool."

He laughed. "Not particularly. We might not have the moonlight thing, but we can't change when we want to. And when we do change, it's kinda… fuzzy."

"Fuzzy? What, like memory-wise?"

"No." Pulling his phone from his pocket, he played around with it for a moment before passing it over. "Watch this."

A short video played. It was a montage of six apparent thylacine sightings over the last ten years.

In each one, you could see a dark shape, mostly in the far distance, of an animal running away. It was hard to be sure they were thylacines. They could have been anything. Except, I also saw the silvery ghost-like human images running after them. More like jogging. I was quite surprised they kept up at the speed the thylacines were going.

"And?"

He pointed at the phone. "Play the last section back, but I want you to pay close attention to the camera work."

The last video was a news reporter at the site of a car accident, and the animal ran out from behind one of the cars and off into the nearby bush.

"I don't know what I'm supposed to notice."

"The first five sightings are shot by amateurs, on phones and whatnot. The camera work is all shaky and they jerk around when they're trying to follow the thylacine. This last one. It's professional. The camera is good quality, and everything else is in sharp focus. Everything but the thylacine. It's fuzzy."

I played it back, this time paying careful attention to the detail. Josh was right. Everything else was clear. Nothing else went out of focus. Nothing except the thylacine... and the silver ghost human, but it was normal for the ghost part to be hazy.

"So... what? The thylacine is fuzzy, like out of focus?"

"Yes."

Tilting my head, I tried to remember when I'd seen Josh at the bottom of the landslide in thylacine form. "That's right. You were blurry. Why?"

Josh shook his head. "Don't know. No one

does."

"It couldn't have always been like that. I mean, the video of the last thylacine in captivity back in the thirties was clear as anything. Well, as clear as film was in those days. Even if they did name it Benjamin when there was a woman connected to it."

Josh turned to stare at me. Literally, he shifted in his seat.

I waited for a second, but he continued to stare. "What?"

"What do you mean 'a woman connected to it'?"

"Exactly what I said."

He continued to frown at me as though I had two heads.

I tried again. "You know, the silver ghostly thing. You're the one who guessed I could see it. Why is it such a big surprise now?"

"Let me get this straight. When you look at me, you can see a silver ghostly thylacine, but when you look at a thylacine, you can see a silver ghostly... human?"

"Yes," I confirmed slowly. "Why? Is that strange?"

"This whole thing is strange." His breath came out in a rush as he shoved his untied hair back.

"Tell me about it," I muttered.

"It would make sense, I suppose. I've never considered it before. So, when I shifted, you could see me as a silver ghostly... whatever?"

"Yep."

He seemed pretty laid back about being naked when he shifted from thylacine to human, but I was pretty sure he wouldn't want to know his ghostly self was naked, too, though it was a temptation to tease him about it to see how he'd react.

His eyebrows shot up. "I guess you see what we feel."

"What do you feel?"

"It's kinda hard to explain, but when I'm in human form, I can feel the beast… here." He tapped the top of his stomach, directly on his solar plexus. "But it's more than a feeling. I'm aware. My senses are normal human senses. There's nothing extraordinary about them at all, but it's like there's something extra. Not from how I perceive things, but from the beast within."

"And when you're thylacine?"

Josh closed his eyes for a second. "Not sensory as in touch or sight or anything, but more a deeper conceptual awareness."

"So, whatever form you are, the other form can still think and feel?"

"No, I don't. Like, there's not two consciousnesses in my head or anything. It's more of an overall… awareness. That's the best I can do. I can't really explain it."

"That's okay. I think I get it. Are you going to eat those?"

"What?" He glanced down at where my finger was pointing at his cardboard cup of chips and shook his head. "No, they're all yours."

"You said before that you can't change whenever you want. What's the trigger?"

He tilted his head and stared out over the view for a few seconds. "I guess adrenaline would probably be the best answer. It's almost a flight-or-fight response. But even when that thin sliver of a window opens and you can touch the beast, it's like swimming against the current in a river of mud. It's so hard to keep connected."

"So, not all fun and games, hey?"

He gave a faint smile at that. "No."

I suppose I should have been freaking out about everything he was telling me. Being able to change from a human to an animal was the stuff of movies and horror novels. All I felt was relief. I wasn't crazy, and I didn't have ghost thylacine suddenly deciding to follow me. They were attached to them. And they were real. Kind of. Well, at least they had a plausible reason to be there. In a way.

I wasn't the only one who knew about them, even if I was the only one who could apparently see them. I cut myself off before I could convince myself my relief at seeing the ghostly animals was another example of the fact I was actually crazy.

"I guess that makes us even." I shook the last of the chips from the packet and tossed the red cardboard into the paper bag with the rest of the rubbish.

"What does?"

"I know your secret and you know mine."

"What secret?"

"You're a theri... shifter."

He scoffed at me. "Therianthrope. I meant what secret of yours do I know?"

I tilted my head at him for a moment, waiting for him to make the connection, and when he didn't, I mimed drawing with my left hand.

"You do draw the future." He grinned for a second. "I knew it. Does anyone else know? I mean besides your family, obviously."

"Not even my family."

"What? Why not?"

I sucked on the straw of my thick-shake,

stalling. This was a part of my life I didn't share with anyone, but fair was fair. Carefully, I put the drink into the cup holder and leaned back in the seat.

"For the first few years, I didn't realise what I did was anything special. I thought everyone did what I did. It was only when others told me how wonderful my drawings were that I discovered I could draw better than anyone my age. It was just a talent I had. Some people sing. Some people sew. I draw. At first, nothing seemed out of the ordinary. A few things happened, like drawing ten dollars lying on the street, and the next day finding it exactly where I drew it. That kind of thing. I didn't know it wasn't 'normal.' It was just life. You know?"

"It would be, if no one told you any differently. How old were you when it started?"

"I can't remember. Mum said I picked up a pencil before I could crawl, so maybe then? I don't know." I shrugged and sighed. "One day, I drew two pictures of my stepfather, Shane. One was of his car at a funny angle at the side of the road with a dead kangaroo in the middle of the street. The other… well, I thought I drew him sleeping."

Josh winced. "I think I can see where this is going."

"Yeah. Well, when I left for school that day, I told him he had to be careful about kangaroos. I don't know what he thought of that. He didn't mention it when I came home, and neither did I. In fact, it wasn't spoken of again."

"He died after hitting a kangaroo."

I nodded even though it wasn't a question. "About eight months after I drew the pictures. He was texting on his phone while driving. There weren't any skid marks, according to the cops. A hundred kilometres an hour directly into a kangaroo. I didn't go to the funeral. I had chicken pox. Four or five months later, Mum found the drawings. She freaked out. An eight-year-old shouldn't be drawing car crashes and dead people, apparently. I told her I'd drawn them before Shane had died, but she didn't believe me. She thought it was some deep-seated grief I had and I was lying—I don't know, for attention or something. That started two years of visits with a shrink. At first, I told the truth, but that got me put on medication. So, I pretended I had made it up. That I did want attention. That having three sisters with another one on the way at the time—she was born before I finished the visits—made me feel like I was being lost in the crowd. Finally, they dropped the meds. A few months later, I didn't have to go back to visit the shrink. And I never told anyone again. Until now."

I thought I'd done pretty well, but tears had started part way through and were trailing silently down my face. Reaching across to the glove box, Josh pulled out a tissue box and handed it me.

"I believe you."

His voice was low in the dark interior of the car, and for some reason, I nearly lost it. Hiding my face in the tissue, I took slow, deep breaths. The tears didn't want to stop, and I struggled with keeping it together. Josh didn't say anything else. He didn't try to shush me or comfort me. He sat silently in the driver seat until I could pull myself together. Even after I threw the used tissues into the paper bag with the rest of the rubbish, he remained silent. I stared out over the view for a while, trying to sift through the things he'd told me already. I needed to focus on something else right now, not my past.

"Are thylacine the only shifters?"

Thankfully, he took the change of subject and ran with it. "America, Africa, Europe, Ireland, China—they all have them."

"Tasmanian tigers are all over the world?" That was new.

"No. Each country has their own beasts. Wolves, bears, dodos, deer, marten, otters… you name it. Australia has three, apparently. Dingoes, devils, and us."

My eyes widened in shock. Not that I'd ever seen a dingo or a Tasmanian devil for real, and to the best of my memory, I'd never seen one as a silver ghost either.

"Tasmanian tigers and Tasmanian devils? Two out of three ain't bad."

"Three out of three. Dingoes were in Tasmania too, back when Tasmania was connected to the mainland instead of separated by water."

"Whoa. That had to be a long time ago. So, are you guys Aboriginal?"

Josh shook his head. "Not Australian Aboriginal at any rate. Mum and a few other family members got themselves DNA tested for ancestry a few years back. Apparently, there are no noticeable differences to origins compared to non-therianthropes. No one knows for sure where they come from, how they came to be, or even pinpoint exactly when, but there are thylacine depicted in Aboriginal cave art going back centuries."

"So, your family has been around for a while."

"Apparently."

Opening the glove box, I put the tissues away

and noticed a pink blur across my vision. My first reaction was to hide my left hand between the car seat and the door so I could flex it, unseen. I was halfway through the motion when I realised I didn't have to hide it. Not with Joshua. That felt weird.

"Can you reach my bag in the back?"

Josh shifted in the seat and leaned between the seats to collect my bag, only to stop moving partway through and stare at me.

"What?"

He shook his head. "Your eyes are so purple right now it's eerie."

"Yeah, I need to draw."

Josh handed my bag over. "Draw the future?"

I shrugged. "Probably."

There was one good thing about Joshua's tendency to stay silent. He didn't talk at all while I was drawing, although I was very much aware he was watching me the entire time.

"A book? Is it some kind of spell book?" Joshua took the sketchbook while I put the pencil away.

I looked across at the drawing. It was of a distinctly female hand holding a book with jumbled letters across the pages. "Nah. It'll be just a book."

"A book with code." He frowned and whispered the words again, almost like it triggered a memory or something. "A book with code."

"No, a book with writing."

"You draw writing with crazy, unreadable words often?"

I shook my head. "That's how I see words."

"Where do you see words like that?"

"Every time I read."

"What?"

"I'm dyslexic."

With a frown, he slowly lifted his head to look at me. "Dyslexic?"

"My brain confuses the letters on the page and they look like they're moving."

"I know what dyslexia is. I should have expected it, but I didn't."

"Expected it?"

"It's one of the indicators."

His phone rang as he spoke, and he took it out to answer. I retrieved my sketchbook. My dyslexia was connected to me drawing the future? That was weird. I wasn't sure if I was freaked out by it or comforted. There was a fine line.

"I have to go." Josh's tone was tight as he tossed the phone into the centre console and started the car.

"Go?"

"Something has come up at home."

"Human something, or thylacine something?"

He glanced at me, pausing for a moment in reversing. "Don't know. Ginny, you can't tell anyone about what I've told you. Not even my family."

"It's such a big secret from them, because…?"

"Finding a Seer is a big thing. If you are one, then everything in our world is about to change. If you're not one, then I've broken the Therianthrope Code."

Chapter Nine

"And to end the day, your assignments are now marked. I'll give you the last few minutes to go to your grades folder... and have a good weekend."

I closed my eyes as Mr Goss went back to his desk. It had taken him weeks to mark them but I didn't want to see my grade. This was the first English assignment I'd submitted in more than a year. If previous experience was anything to go by, I was pretty sure there'd be a big fat D on the assignment... or whatever the lowest grade was here. I didn't need to look at it. Even if I had worked hard on it, I was pretty sure it wouldn't change the status quo.

"How'd it go?" Surprised, I looked up at Evie. She was leaning back on her chair again so she could rest her weight on her arm across my desk. She was lucky I didn't have a thing about personal space. "On your assignment?"

I shrugged.

"You haven't checked yet?"

"No."

"Why not?"

"Don't really care."

"For real?"

"The book was boring."

"I completely agree and I inhale books. This one was so hard to read and keep interested."

"Tell me about it," I muttered.

She shook her head and ran her other hand through her hair, deliberately mussing the short, blonde pixie haircut so it danced like a halo around her head.

"I usually get As in English, but this time I got a B. Apparently, I spent too much time discussing character relationships and not enough on themes."

"Okay."

Evie seemed nice and was obviously friendly, but for some reason, I had no idea what to say to her, even if I was pretty sure she wanted to compare grades. There was something about her I couldn't put my finger on. It was like she was overkill friendly in short, sharp bursts, almost like she was trying too hard.

"Did you really not check your grade?"

"Yes... no? Which answer means I didn't check?"

"Well, are you going to?"

"Not planning to, no."

"Why not?"

"I know I suck at English. I don't need a letter of the alphabet to prove it."

"You can't mean that."

"Why does it matter to you, anyway?"

"I want to see if Goss is being hard on everyone or just me."

"You can ask Helen." I tilted my head toward

Evie's actual friend, sitting on the other side of her, talking to the girl in front of her, whose name I'd forgotten. The whole room was washed in gradually increasing sounds of conversation now that Goss had given us the few minutes before the bell.

"She got an A, so it doesn't help."

"So maybe you just got a B. It happens."

"If you don't want to tell me what you got, can you at least tell me if it was higher or lower than you expected?"

That made me laugh. It couldn't possibly be lower. "Fine."

Moving the cursor on the screen, I clicked the link to the Grades page then navigated to the most recent grade for English. It took a second for the page to open, and when it did, I could only stare.

"Well, is it higher or lower?"

"Higher." I was in shock as I turned to face her. "Much, much higher. I got a B+."

"What do you normally get?"

"Ds."

"Really?"

"Yeah."

"Then it is definitely just me. Congratulations, by the way."

"Thanks."

I turned back to the screen. The B+ didn't move or jump around. It wasn't a figment of my imagination. Eighty-four percent.

The bell ringing snapped me from the hypnotising hold of the rounded letter. I had to wait for the rush of students to leave the classroom before I grabbed my crutches. I'd only been on them for three weeks and already I was sick of them. I had another three weeks to go until the next doctor visit before I even had the chance to get rid of them.

"Mr Goss?"

"Yes?"

"About my grade—"

I snuck out of there while Evie had him cornered. I didn't want him to see me and realise he'd given me someone else's grade in error. At least not yet. I wanted to enjoy the B+ for a little while longer.

The walk to the car park usually took forever on my crutches at the end of the day. Today, I made it to the fence before I realised it. I couldn't see Dad's car. Great, I would have to sit on the icy cold concrete steps unless I wanted to continue balancing my weight between my good leg and the crutches that were already rubbing my armpits raw despite the padding and my layers of clothes.

I'd just braved the freezing stone on my backside, when I heard a car horn and recognised Josh's car. It drove closer, but it wasn't Josh driving.

"Cornelia?"

Cautiously, I approached the car. It had been two weeks since Josh had pulled his disappearing act on our "date" but his worry about his family finding out must have rubbed off on me, because seeing his mother made me feel like I was in trouble.

"Hi, Ginny. Your dad sent me to pick you up today. He has to work late."

Struggling with my bag, I pulled it around to find my phone. As much as I knew Cornelia was probably not dangerous or anything, I was pretty sure Dad would have let me know. Sure enough, there was a text from him. I was to have dinner with the Borradailes and he'd pick me up later tonight.

"How'd you get off scot-free?" I asked her as she took my crutches so I could get into the passenger side.

"I've taken the last two sick duties. It was his turn."

"Fair enough."

She had the heater on, and I could feel the cold seeping out of me. It wasn't fair the cold froze me in seconds but it took heaters forever to warm me up. Unlike Dad's old Land Rover, this car was a sleek and silver 4-wheel drive SUV. It kind of looked like a fat shark with a snarling grill. The badge on the front was a sharp 'L' in an oval, and I reckon it might normally have been a comfortable car, but with a cast, it was awkward. Cornelia's thylacine sat up in the back seat, staring at me. It barely moved. In fact, it barely blinked. It was freaking me out. Hers had the same deep, soul-dark eyes as Josh's, and when they were aimed directly at me, there was a hypnotic pulling power. For a second, I thought it was my imagination, but it wasn't. The thylacine was trembling.

"Are you okay?" I frowned at Cornelia as I remembered Josh's running like a puppy spiked with red cordial. If there was a connection between the thylacine and the human, it was entirely possible it expressed the actual emotional state of its human. Cornelia was the one freaking out.

"Yes. Why?" Her answer was super-fast.

"I don't know. You seem kinda tense."

"Tense? No." She laughed. "Not at all."

Her thylacine began to pace the backseat. It was a little freaky to see it in the side mirror of the car phasing half through the back door as he turned in its pacing By the time we reached the edge of town, it had its head on the centre console and was staring at me. Something had to be going on here.

"How was school?" Cornelia blurted.

"Pretty good. I got my first B+ in English."

"That's great. Great."

Leaning closer to the door, I narrowed my eyes at her. She was no longer the casual lady on the train. Her hands kept twisting forward and backwards on the steering wheel, like she couldn't keep them still. When she saw me looking at her, she flicked me a grin then darted her eyes back to the road. There was only one thing I could think of for the change, and if I was right, then Josh had told his family about me. I didn't say anything. If I was reading this wrong and Josh hadn't, I didn't want to get him into trouble. I stared out of the window instead. At least this way, I couldn't see her thylacine staring at me. I could feel its eyes boring into my head. It was almost a relief when she tapped the radio button on her steering wheel.

The trip was longer than I thought it would be, and we went all the way out into the Tyndall Regional Reserve. It sure as hell wasn't just a 'few kilometres over that ridge.' That was for sure. But then, I'd already figured out Josh had lied. After all, Dad had mentioned Josh had arrived at the house on a motorbike. Not walked. That motorbike had to have been parked somewhere close by for him to go back and get it before reporting the landslide. Tyndall Regional Reserve was near Cradle Mountain. Well, nearer than we were, at any rate. I didn't even think it was legal for people to live out here.

As comfortable as the car was, dirt roads were

dirt roads, and the jolting was starting to make my leg ache. To take my mind off it, I looked out at the trees as classical music tinkled from the radio. I couldn't get over how green everything was here. Tall, grey, and olive green, the gum trees reached for the clouds with their skeletal branches, whispering with their narrow leaves glistening with heavy, fat raindrops. They towered like watchmen in a swirling crowd of more trees, bushes, tall grasses, tangled indeterminate vines, and ground cover. I could easily imagine the trees grasping for the car and pulling it in, absorbing us like water in a sponge.

"Here we are."

Cornelia turned off the dirt road at a driveway marked by half tires with red reflectors curved along their sides. The driveway had to be longer than ours. The further in we went, the taller the trees grew. It went from a pretty avenue style, to an honest to goodness forest. The branches were so thick overhead Cornelia turned on her headlights, and we could have been in the deepest, darkest parts of the Amazon. When the house finally came into view, it wasn't anything I expected. Dark stone stairs with a thick, white cement balustrade led up to a house that was red brick at the bottom and white with black wood chocolate-box trim on the second level. The red brick level had a bay window on the left and an enclosed porch on the right. The weird thing was the white level overhung the red level by about a meter with no posts or anything to hold it up. She pulled into one of the garages detached from the house. It was one of a line of five double garages, glaringly modern compared to the house. The garages held two cars, a bike, and an entire workshop on the far right covering two bays.

"Interesting house."

"It was built in the early 1800s." Cornelia held my crutches so I could slide out of the passenger seat.

"I guess that's kinda cool."

She shut the car door for me and indicated to the black motorbike in the next bay. "Josh's bike. Means he's home. We'll go around the back. There are no stairs."

"Josh owns a bike and a car? Wow."

"No, only the bike. The car's mine."

We went around the side and through the back. The back door opened out into a small tiled area with hooks for jackets, a mirrored stand, and so many shoes lined against the wall it looked like a giant centipede lived here. The keys in Cornelia's green handbag clinked as she set it on the small table then removed her coat. I could hear conversations floating from somewhere further in the house.

"Is there some kind of gathering?"

"Just Josh and Monty, I'd say... and from the sounds of it, Barbara, too. Do you want to take off your jacket?"

"I'm fine." It was too much of a juggling act with my backpack and the crutches.

Cornelia waved with her hand for me to follow her down the hallway. "Do you drink coffee?"

"Herbal tea?"

"I think we have green tea. Do you want some?"

"Sure."

Her thylacine raced down the hallway then bounded back again. It stood close to the wall, and up ahead, where a wide archway with a railed wooden fence divided the room, three thylacines peered out. The one that checked us out and disappeared again, I recognised as Josh's. There was just something in the way the thylacine tilted its head. The other two stayed where they were staring at me. One of them lifted its head as I approached, and as much as an animal face could show expression, I was pretty sure it was staring at me in amazement. Of course, I could be imagining it. But with one tearing around the house like a tiny whirlwind and the other two staring fixedly at me, it was far too easy to let my imagination take over. At least Josh's was calm and settled, from what I could see of it from out in the hall.

Cornelia walked through the thylacine in the doorway like it wasn't there, and I had to laugh at myself. I'd been worried about hitting the marsupials with my crutches as I tried to squeeze past them. They weren't really there; I could walk through them. As I did, I wondered if I was the only one who could feel the heat from their ghostly bodies, or if everyone else could too. I wasn't sure I could ask.

"Ginny, this is my husband, Monty." Cornelia gestured towards an older man and I didn't need the TARDIS tie to connect the dots.

"You're the teacher."

He gave a short laugh. "Yes, I am."

Cornelia continued her introductions. "And this is my daughter, Barbara."

Barbara wore a cherry red, snug-fitting '50s pin-up dress with large white polka dots this time. I didn't need her black bob or the awesome ink down her arm and leg to recognise her. She was the owner of the Painted Serpent.

I paused so I could give a wave. "Hi."

"This is yours." Barbara tapped the table, and I saw my portfolio under her hand.

"Oh, great. Thanks." I was more relieved than I realised, considering I never bothered to chase it up.

"They're pretty good."

"Good enough to get me a job?"

She gave a huff of laughter. "Depends."

"On...?"

"On whether you can draw like this all the time, or only when the... mood... strikes."

There was a peculiar tone to her voice when she said the word *mood*. With narrowed eyes, I looked at each of them one at a time. I didn't know them well enough to be sure, but from watching the thylacines, I was getting a distinctive vibe of anticipation. Suspiciously, I turned to Josh and gave him a pointed look.

"Josh confirmed it, but that wasn't what gave you away."

I turned back to Barbara. "Gave what away?"

"Drawing the future."

My first instinct was to deny it, but I figured it was a useless ploy. "Uh-huh. So, what did?"

Barbara opened my portfolio and pushed it across the table toward me. The drawing was of a vista of rooftops and mingle of trees depicting a small town rising up to meet the mountains in the distance.

"A landscape. Wow, so futuristic."

"Except it is the exact view from the window of my flat above the Painted Serpent. All but this." She pointed to a large building to the left of the picture. "This is a construction site right now."

"Artistic licence, drawing what I thought would be there."

"Construction only started two weeks ago. You've never been to my flat to see this view, and even if you Googled it, it would still show the three warehouses that used to be there."

"Okay." I glared at Josh. "Considering some of the other things I'd drawn of the future in the past, this seems a little forced. Josh, what did you tell them?"

"Ginny, I—"

With a slow smile, Barbara stood from her chair. "He's telling the truth. You can draw the future."

"What happened to not telling anyone, not even your family?" I asked Josh.

"Don't blame him," Cornelia told me. "We didn't give him much choice."

"You held a gun to his head?"

"I wouldn't let him have the Chronicle until he told me why he wanted it."

"Say what now?"

Cornelia gestured toward the table. "How about you take a seat. I'll grab your tea and we can sort this all out."

Slowly, I sat.

"Relax." Monty spoke for the first time. "We're not going to do anything untoward."

They probably wanted answers as much as I did, but I didn't want to go twenty rounds to get there.

"How about we drop the games and be honest with each other?" I nodded at Barbara. "I'm pretty sure you hadn't even opened my portfolio until— and correct me if I'm wrong—Josh pointed it out.

I'm guessing as an attempt to prove to you that I apparently draw the future."

"Oh yeah? What makes you say that?" she challenged me.

"If you'd looked at it sooner, we'd have had this conversation long before now."

Monty leaned back in his chair with a smile. "Fair call."

"You want to know what other indicators I show, and I want to know more about ther... ther... shifters."

Cornelia entered the room, carrying a tray of mugs.

"Therianthrope," Monty supplied. "How long have you known?"

"A little longer than you've known about me, apparently, although the first thylacine I saw was Barbara's at the Painted Serpent."

"Silvers." Cornelia twisted to place the tray on the hutch behind her. "The representation of our beasts that you see are called Silvers. And I'm willing to bet you found out about us the same way we found out about you." She sent a questioning glance towards Josh.

"What else could I do, Mum? She'd seen me Beast Walk."

"Whoa, hold up." Barbara held up her hands. "I didn't know that happened."

"We didn't either, until the other week, after he'd told Ginny about us." Monty didn't sound too impressed.

Barbara looked shocked, and she blinked a few times before wiping her hand in an 'erase that' motion. "I did not hear that. If anyone asks, Ginny, you found out today, right now. Got it?"

"Why?"

"Dad and I are Elders on the council. We have authority to speak of therianthropes. Josh does not. There are dire consequences for those who speak of it and don't have the authority."

"Such as?"

"Best scenario, banishment. As for the worst, let's not even go there."

"They haven't killed anyone for breaking the code in decades." Josh stared down into his mug.

"That's because it hasn't been broken in decades." Monty didn't sound like he was joking.

I sat up. "Killed? Seriously?"

Barbara frowned. "Yes."

"So, what you're telling me, Monty and Barbara, is the ghost thylacines I've been seeing are a representation of the beasts you can shift into. I can see them, because it's possible I'm a Seer. If I am a Seer, then there are indicators that will prove it. Like the fact I'm dyslexic and can draw the future."

Monty have a short laugh. "Good girl."

"One of the indicators is to predict the future, not necessarily draw it," Barbara corrected me.

"What are the other indicators?"

"Predict the future." Monty counted off on his fingers. "Inability to read. See Silvers. Speak a second language instinctively from birth. Come from a line of Seers. And be female."

I counted on my fingers back at him. "Yes, yes, yes, no, haven't got the foggiest, and yes."

"You don't speak a second language?"

"Not that I'm aware of."

"And it's speak a language instinctively from birth, Dad. Not a second one. Did you start speaking

94

from a very, very early age, like days old?" Barbara asked.

Josh nodded. "Because if you instinctively speak English, that could completely happen."

I shrugged. "I have no idea. It's not something Mum ever told me if I did."

"You could have spoken it, but if it was a foreign language, everyone could have thought it was baby babble. We'll have to listen to you for a while and see if you randomly throw in an odd word now and then, to figure it out." Barbara ran her finger over the handle of her coffee mug, apparently thinking out loud. "Who was your grandmother on your mother's side?"

"Dawn Martin. I don't know what her maiden name was. She died when I was two."

"Where was she born?"

I glanced at Cornelia. "Bundaberg."

"It's possible." Monty crossed his arms. "The last Seer had two boys. One had a son, and the other had no children. The son left Tasmania in 1944, and we can't find him."

"And you think my grandmother is related to him?"

"If you're a Seer, then yes."

"If this whole Seer thing is hereditary, you'd think Mum would have told me something, right?"

Monty shook his head. "While Seers always follow a family line, it's not directly generational. Firstborn granddaughter to firstborn granddaughter, missing the second generation. Even if you're a Seer, your mother wouldn't be."

"And if your grandmother died when you were two, it would explain why no one was there to tell you before now," Barbara added.

Sitting back in the chair, I cradled my teacup to my chest—the hot china had already cooled to warm—and had to take a minute for all this to sink in. "And if I am a Seer, what then? I'm the same as I was, except I can now see thylacine ghosts? Sorry… Silvers, right? It's not like I have to suddenly kill vampires or defeat the meanest, baddest warlock in the world or anything?"

"No killing." Monty smiled briefly. "But there is something."

Carefully, I placed the cup on the table, just in case the "something" was horrendous. I didn't want to start breaking their crockery. "Okay."

"Canis lupus dingo and sarcophagus harrisii can Beast Walk whenever they want to. Not so with the thylacines."

My eyebrows lifted at the gobbledygook that left Monty's mouth. "Canis… what and who now?"

"Dingoes and devils," Josh translated.

I shook my head. I thought the word thylacine was bad. At least it was pronounceable… now that I had the hang of it, anyway. That sarcoph-a-thingy sounded like a swear word. Or at least a hairy sarcophagus.

"Thylacines can only Beast Walk when there is danger," Monty continued.

"I'm assuming 'Beast Walk' is when you shift?"

Monty frowned for a second. "Yes, I suppose it can be called shifting."

"A Seer is the only one who can fix it. Make it so we can Beast Walk at will." Barbara obviously thought Monty was taking too long.

"How's that supposed to happen?"

Barbara shrugged. "We don't know."

"But that's why I was asking Mum about the Chronicle."

I looked across at Josh. The only thing I knew about Chronicles was that Narnia apparently had them. "What's a Chronicle?"

"A book written by Seers for Seers. It's their passed down knowledge." Cornelia stood and left the room. No one spoke until she returned with a red fabric-covered book. She placed it in front of me. "Rachel left this behind on a visit once, and she died before we could give it back."

"And Rachel is…?"

"The last Seer." Cornelia sat back down. "It's one of her Chronicles. The notebooks left from Seer to Seer to record all the important information. This is only one of them. Allegedly, there are many, many more, but they were lost after Rachel died."

"I thought Seers couldn't read. Why would they write notebooks of information?"

"Seers have been around longer than computers. They had to record their knowledge somehow."

"Well, that sucks." I opened to a random page and pressed the soft book open at the spine, sliding my fingers down the left-hand page. The words were even more letter switched than normal, though strangely the letters stayed in the same place even as my gaze passed over the words.

"Particularly when it is some sort of code none of us can read," Cornelia told me.

Josh leaned across and peered at the pages. I handed him the book.

He frowned as he turned pages. "Hey, Ginny. You know what this looks like, don't you?"

"A book?"

"The drawing of the spell-code book you did in the car the other week."

It was my turn to frown as I gestured with my hand that I wanted him to pass the book back to me. As I turned the book around to bring it the right way, I experienced a severe case of déjà vu. A female hand holding a book of jumbled words. Josh was right. It was the exact same moment I'd drawn.

"You have to stop doing that," I muttered.

"Doing what?"

"Pointing out the reality of my drawings moments before I see it myself. The train, this. It's freaking me out."

"I think it's cool." Josh grinned.

Cornelia leaned closer. "Can you read it?"

This time, I studied the words. Each individual word was impossible to make out. It was a jumble of letters. But when I ran my eyes quickly over the page, a complete sentence jumped out at me.

"Parliament ruled today. Finally, the fight is over. Finally, the... something... *is free from... persecution?* I think that's the word."

"You can read it?" Josh moved around the table until he sat next to me and peered down at the page.

With a frown, I attempted the sentence again. *"Finally, the fight is over. Finally, the theri... theri...."*

"Therianthrope?" Cornelia guessed.

"Possibly? It's a bloody long word, whatever it is."

"How the hell can you read that?" Barbara asked.

I shrugged. "It's just there."

"What parliament ruling do you think it's talking about?" Josh twisted to ask his mother.

"Does it mention a date?"

I couldn't find one on the page and flipped back a few pages. "Yeah. April 26th, 1909."

Cornelia shook her head. "It doesn't ring any bells to me."

I flipped back to the page I'd read before. "*Finally, the theri-*whatsit *is free from persecution. It is time to undo what has been done.*"

"What was done?" Cornelia leaned forward in her seat.

I shrugged and turned the page, moving my eyes over the words again until they made sense.

"*This is my first entry....* Huh? Well the handwriting is different, and it's dated... 2nd of March, 1926. That's what, thirteen or so years later?" I looked up at the Borradailes. Cornelia nodded but didn't say anything. All of them looked at me expectantly. I kept reading. "*This is my first entry, and I must first explain Prudence Chesney passed from this world in 1910, on September 9th. She was brutally murdered in her home, and the killer has yet to be brought to justice.*"

"Prudence must have been the previous Seer," Cornelia mused.

"Rachel's grandmother? I mean, this is Rachel's book, right?" I flicked to the inside front cover, looking for a name or something. I didn't find anything. I tucked my hair behind my ear and glanced back down to the page. "*Her death has left a gap in knowledge. I have read the Chronicles and cannot find or understand how the Beasts are Lashed. I will not give up. I will find a way. While the Silvers are still...* opa... que—"

"O-pa-cue. What's that?" Josh frowned at me. I shrugged.

"Read the rest of it. Context may give us a clue." Cornelia whirled her finger to get me to keep reading.

"*While the Silvers are still… that… there is hope. I will find the answer before they evanesce.*"

"Before they what now?" Josh sounded as confused as I was.

"Evanesce. To be forgotten. Disappear from memory."

"Disappear?" I frowned. "Your Silvers are translucent. Like ghosts."

"Translucent?" Cornelia snapped her fingers. "Opaque, not o-pa-cue. The opposite of translucent."

"So… what? We're too late? They're already disappearing?"

"You can still see them, right?" Josh pointed at me.

"Yeah."

"So, they haven't disappeared yet. There's still time… hope… whatever."

"What the hell is a…" I flicked my eyes back over the words, looking for the one in particular. "Lashed? As in how the beasts are Lashed?"

Cornelia shook her head. "I don't know. But from the sounds of it, I'd say it has something to do with why we can't Beast Walk easily."

"And 1926? Looks like Rachel was trying to figure it out for a really long time. What makes you think I can do what she couldn't?"

"Because you draw the future." Cornelia made it sound like she'd announced the answer to the universe.

"And?"

"From what I know of other Seers, they saw the

future in dreams and visions. You draw it. You are the only one to have evidence of the predictions. You can go back and look at them again and again. Look for details a simple rendition might miss."

"Bring your sketchbooks here next time," Josh told me. "You read the Chronicle, and we'll comb through your drawings. Maybe we'll find connections or missed clues. I mean, you did say yourself that I'm good at pointing out when the drawings are real. With all of us looking, surely one of us has to be able to help you find the answer."

"And what if I haven't drawn it?"

"What if you have?" Barbara's tone was low. "Dad, I think we need to run this past the Elders and see what they say, but I think Josh is on to something."

I could only stare. Not only did they believe the drawings were predictions of the future, but they believed they could be important. I was stunned and, if I was honest, more freaked out about it than I was at finding out shifters were real.

Chapter Ten

Pulling down the last of the photos, I dumped the small pile of bits into the plastic zip-lock bag on my desk. Now that I had most of the answers, I didn't need my mind map on the wall. Standing there, I placed my hand on the small red book still on my desk.

The Seer Chronicle.

Sounded like some B-grade, kid's afternoon TV show.

Picking it up, I flicked through the slightly crinkled and yellowed pages, opening to one at random. I had practically memorised it over the past few weeks since the Borradailes had given it to me, but reading it wasn't my goal. I'd tried all afternoon to figure out how to write the code and came up blank. If I glanced over it, I could read it, but if I focused on the letters, they didn't make words. I could read "the" in two different sentences. The first time the letters came together as "roc," the next time "xns." They both said "the," but I didn't know why. When I wrote the letters on a blank page to try to figure it out, they became a random bunch of letters. I couldn't read them. It was worse than trying to read normally. It was like the words only became words because they were read from the book. Maybe it was some magic spell book after all. If you'd told me a few months ago I'd seriously be considering an old journal-type book was imbued with magical powers, I would have called you crazy. Now… anything was possible.

I wanted to record my part of the story. It felt like a responsibility I needed to undertake. There were no pages left in this book, but it didn't mean I couldn't start one of my own. If Rachel died twenty-something years ago, then there couldn't have been a record since then. An audio recording was out of the question, as was writing it down in normal English. I didn't grow up with five sisters without knowing anything could be found and used against you. Which was why, even with Dad as the only other person living in this house, I was being extra careful with the Chronicle. It was usually stored in a plastic bag taped to the back of my bedside table.

What I wanted to do was find the other Chronicles. If there were more of them, then I could learn what 'Lashing' the beast was. It would be so cool to watch Josh and his family shift whenever they wanted to. It wasn't fair that devils and dingoes could, but they couldn't.

I ran my thumb over the edge of the pages, fanning the book from the back end to the front. I don't even know why I did it. Something to do while I thought, I suppose. As I bent the back cover to do it again, a strange crinkling sound stopped me. I ran my hand over the outside of the back cover. Nothing. Opening to the last page, I ran my hand over the inside of the back cover this time. It was the tiniest bump, but I felt it. Something was inside the back cover. Inspecting it more closely, I saw that an extra sheet of paper, cut to size, had been glued to the back cover. Finding the scissors in my desk drawer, I carefully pried the corner of the suspicious rectangle. Not by much, but enough that I could use the scissors to pull a folded square of paper free. It smelt musty as I unfolded it.

"*On the other hand*," I read the coded words out loud. "On the other hand… what?"

That was pretty random to be hidden away in the back of the Chronicle. Pulling the back cover back as far as I could without ripping it, I peered into the depths and felt along it to make sure there wasn't a second hidden scrap. There wasn't.

With a frown, I looked up from the book and turned my head to the front of the house. I could hear an engine. It wasn't far away and on the road; it was close. It didn't sound like a car. It was more open and burbled, rather than rumbled, as it slowed and stopped. Dad's car didn't sound like that, and there was no sound of the garage door opening. Expecting the doorbell, I quickly slid the folded page back into the cover and placed the book into the bag with the photos before sliding the whole thing in the small alcove at the back of my bedside table, repositioning the tape over the edges to keep it in place. Hopefully that would keep it hidden well enough from prying eyes. I stood only to nearly walk through the silver thylacine that had slunk into my room.

It stood there looking up at me.

I sighed. At least the Silvers gave me warning of impending shifter visitors. Moving slowly around the bed, I stared down at the beast again, just to be sure. It blinked as it looked at me. Yep, I was pretty sure I recognised it. In two strides, I crossed to the window and flung aside the curtain. Josh was standing there. With an eye roll, I unlocked the window and pushed it open, shivering in the cold outside air.

"That's not creepy at all." I crossed my arms.

"I didn't know if you'd be home."

"And now you do."

"Can we talk?"

"You expect me to talk to you after dumping the whole thylacine shifter thing on me, then disappearing for two weeks?"

"I was doing research for you." He lifted the satchel at his side. "You won't believe what I've found."

I sighed again. I wanted to be mad at him for some strange reason, but I wasn't. I indicated with my head. "You'd better go around to the front door like a normal human being."

I relocked the window then went through the house, with the thylacine trotting along beside me like a well-trained dog. A large, thigh-high, lanky, feral-looking dog.

"Hey, you've got your cast off." Josh didn't move from the front step.

"Yesterday."

"Is your dad home?"

"No, he went to work about a half hour ago."

"Good." Removing the satchel from his shoulders, he stepped past me into the house.

Shutting the front door, I followed him into the lounge room. "Why good?"

"You are never going to believe what I found

out."

"Obviously shifter related."

"Oh, yeah."

He grabbed papers from the satchel and spread them out on the coffee table as he knelt on the TV side of the table. Taking his lead, I sat cross-legged on the other.

Josh looked up at me. "One of Mum's cousins, Reece, works at the West Coast Council, and she looked up any reference relating to land titles and Rachel Rawdon. While she didn't find Rachel Rawdon, she did find Grace Rawdon. The person who owned the land before Grace was Prudence Chesney."

My head shot up. "Prudence Chesney? That's the name in the Chronicle. The woman who was murdered."

"The Seer who was murdered," Josh corrected me. "But check this out, because this is where it gets interesting. Check out who owns the house now."

He rifled through the pages then pulled one out. Slowly, I looked down to where his finger was pointing, expecting to wade through a hell of a lot of writing, but the name directly at his fingertip jumped out at me.

"That's Dad's name." I pulled the papers closer. "Are you telling me…?"

Josh sat back on his legs and grinned at me. His excitement was contagious. "It would have been easier to find if your last name was the same as his and not your step-fathers, but that's exactly what I'm telling you. The next name on the land title is David Doherty. Your father. Ginny, Rachel's house is your house." He waved a hand around. "This house."

"My father bought Rachel's house? Are you kidding me?"

"No." Josh grinned at me. "The Chronicles were last known to be in this house. You can start looking for them. How cool is that?"

I wasn't so sure I believed him. The coincidence was too uncanny. "You're not having me on? This is real?"

"As real as I am."

"I'm not so sure you are real," I muttered.

My heart pounded. The Chronicles... here? The answers could be so damn close. My eyes flicked around the nearly empty room as if I might suddenly see a neon sign flashing a huge arrow. Dad's style of decorating made hiding things nearly impossible. "Well, they're not in any common areas, I would have found them by now."

"No attic from the looks of it. It's only one level, right?"

"Yeah. No basement or anything. There is the garage though. Dad's workshop."

"Reece gave me blueprints." He pulled more papers from his satchel.

I took them from him and unfolded them. I might not be able to read, but I could understand blueprints. They were drawings of shapes interconnected into visible and easy to understand patterns.

"They might not even be in the house, you know," Josh mused. "You are on acreage."

"Possible." Reading over the measurements, I screwed my face up as I figured out why they didn't make sense at first. It wasn't metric. Like I could translate feet and inches.

"Do you have your phone?"

Josh pulled it out of his pocket. "Yeah, why?"

"I need a measurement converter." I took it from him and pulled one up via Google, going over each measurement to see if anything stood out. It all seemed fine. A normal house with normal dimensions.

Mostly.

I moved the paper closer to make sure I was reading it correctly.

"Josh, how wide do you reckon a clothes hanger is?"

"Don't know. Why?"

"The shared wall between Dad's bedroom and mine, that's the built-in wardrobes. Mine is only just wide enough for hangers."

"And?"

"This says the combined space for the wardrobes is six and a half feet. Two meters. There's no way mine is a meter. So, unless Dad has tons of space to my mingy share, there's something off about it."

"Let's go."

He waited then followed me down the hall. The first thing I did was check Dad's side of the wardrobe. His was more stacked cardboard storage boxes than clothes. Only the right-hand side had hanging space. It looked like he only had about a dozen shirts, and six of them were work uniforms. Leaning in, I felt for the back wall. It was about the same depth as mine. Just over a hanger wide.

"Hang on. I'll be right back." Darting to the garage, I snatched the tape measure. Josh was in the hallway when I came back.

"Felt odd hanging around in there."

"That's okay." I measured the distance into the

wardrobe. "Sixty centimetres."

Next, I went into my room, pushed aside my clothes, and measured.

"Sixty?" He guessed. "It looks the same."

"Yep. Eighty missing, according to the blue prints."

"It's hard to measure the ends of them because one's a hallway wall, and one's an outside wall." He pointed into my wardrobe. "Do you mind?"

I shrugged. "Go for it."

Leaning in, he tapped the wall. Opening the door on the right-hand side, he moved clothes aside and tapped again. "Do you hear a difference?"

"I'm not sure."

"Okay. I'm going to try something. When I tell you, I want you to tap."

I nodded and Josh closed his eyes. His thylacine wandered through me, and I shivered at the change of temperature. It sat in the middle of the wardrobe and intently stared at the back wall. I nearly knelt down beside it to see what it was finding so fascinating.

"Okay, now." Josh's eyes were still closed.

"Are you sensing with your beast or something? Because he's sitting in the wardrobe."

Josh snorted a laugh. "Yes. Sometimes I wish I could see what you see."

"You've got your eyes closed. You can't see anything."

I reached forward and tapped on the wall. The thylacine didn't move. Inching across, I tapped again then repeated until I'd reached the full length of the wardrobe.

"The left-hand side sounds hollow. Let's test your dad's."

His sounded hollow too, only his was on the right, corresponding exactly to there being something hidden behind the adjoining wall.

I stood with my hands on my hips. "Now what?"

"Now we find out how to get into the cavity."

"My room." I pointed. "If we mess it up, it's my room. We move anything here and I don't have a good excuse."

"Fair enough."

I pushed as many clothes across as I could then Josh helped me pull the rest from the wardrobe and dump everying on the bed, including the shoe rack.

"You have a thing for boots?"

I didn't see a problem with that. I only had twenty-four pairs.

"Yep. Comfy and can be dressed up or down. And I can't tell you how glad I am to be out of the cast so I can wear them again."

He shook his head then hunched down in the wardrobe, running his hand along the floor line, up the wall, and then the top of it. Next, he ran the flat of his hand over the walls before turning his attention to the hanging rod. A soft click was the only warning we had before the back wall swung in a little with a slightly musty smell.

My stomach did a somersault. "What did you do?"

"Pushed up on the rod." He indicated into the space. "Ladies first."

For a second, I was tempted, but then shook my head. "Hell no. There could be creepy crawlies and goodness knows what in there."

He laughed then peered through the opening. "It's dark, wherever it goes. Have you got a torch or something?"

All our torches, candles, matches, and spare batteries were in the top drawer of the hutch in the dining room. I collected some spare batteries, too, just in case.

Josh pushed the opening to the left so it sat flush against the end wall, and took the torch to look around. "I want to make sure we can get back out if it shuts on us."

He went in and out a few times then shocked the hell out of me by shutting himself in.

"Josh?"

The wall opened and he leaned back in. "It's okay. I got it. There's a catch just above head height to my left, next to the door. It's like a little hook. Are you ready to go?"

"Absolutely."

"Careful, there are stairs."

The landing could only accommodate one person and was only barely wide enough for us to walk single file. I had one or two centimetres spare on either side of my shoulders, but Josh wasn't so fortunate. He had to pull his shoulders forward like a hunchback, blocking most of the light in front of us. The cool thing was his thylacine, walking behind me, emitted a pale silver glow. Just enough to see when the walls changed from house walls, to wood, to stone and dirt. And it was getting colder. Abruptly, the tight hallway widened. One second, we were squeezed in, and the next, it was wide enough for me to stick my arms out and touch both sides with my hands. Not that I wanted to. Cobwebs lined the stone like delicate lace, and I was trying not to think of how many web makers were lurking in the shadows, ready to pounce. I checked myself over. I didn't have too much web on me from the tight part. Josh must have copped the brunt of that. I shuddered, wondering how many spiders must be crawling all over him. He wasn't concerned about it at all.

"This is amazing. Like one of those lost underground cities on that TV show."

Josh moved the torch light everywhere as we walked. Now that we were out of the narrow tunnel, the space was curved in an arch overhead. Above us was a half dome of interlocking bricks gradually filtering down into a mix of stone slabs and dirt, into completely dirt at the base.

"Whoa." Josh stumbled for a second before he steadied himself. "Should look where I'm going. There are a few more steps here."

These steps were long dirt treads with thin slices of wood framing the edges of the steps. It took about five footsteps to cover the length of one tread before the next step.

"Just think…" Josh stopped walking for a second and shone the torch to the ground. "These footprints in the dirt here were made by Rachel. She died twenty-two years ago, and they look like they could have been made last week."

"It probably hasn't been disturbed since then. I wonder how the air gets in?"

While it was cold and had a slight waft of damp soil, it wasn't musty or long-time-shut-up smelling.

Josh gave a low whistle. "Check it out."

He stopped, but there was plenty of space to peer around him. It was a small room. The torch light didn't show much in one go, but the room opened out like a jigsaw puzzle under the pan of Josh's torch and the glow of his thylacine.

Cupboards and bookshelves lined the three walls to the left, front, and right. The front wall had a huge tapestry of what looked like a silver Celtic knot of some kind, edged with a line of old-style sailing ships. Directly in the middle of the room was a large wooden table. Piles of books and papers were stacked on both sides with a wide empty space in the middle. Two chairs were pushed in, one on either side of the table, ready to be used at the clear space.

"How is it not dusty?"

"You need your eyes checked. There's a hell of a lot of dust here." Josh grinned.

"Yeah, but it's not thick and tacky, like it's been there a while. Look, no cobwebs around the books. Well, not as much as I would expect anyway."

"Maybe your expectations are too high?" He grinned when I glared at him. "Spiders are picky. Who knew?"

I moved around Josh to investigate the cupboard while he approached the table.

"I've got Chronicles."

I glanced behind me at the table. The torchlight shining down over the pile of books, highlighting faded gold lettering on the top book, gave me the strongest sense of déjà vu.

"What's the matter?" Josh moved the light closer to me.

For a second, I was about to shake my head and give the standard "nothing" before I remembered I didn't have to. "A drawing coming true."

"Awesome." Josh grinned. He moved the beam of light into the cupboard I'd opened. "What did you find?"

"Not sure. Metal boxes."

"How can you see over there?"

"Your thylacine glows."

"Really? Cool."

Coming closer, Josh handed me the torch and reached for a box.

"Locked metal boxes. There has to be something interesting in them. They all look the same, and there's about... what... fifteen?"

I did a brief count in the half dark. "About that, yeah."

"Hang on."

Moving to the left, he reached for the wall beside the cupboard, close to the archway we'd come in by. With a soft click, the room was washed with an amber light.

"Would you look at that? Power."

I followed his gaze upwards. Three naked bulbs hung down from the brick arched ceiling, connected by three long, thick cables that travelled back to the switch. Only two of them were working, but they gave off enough light. More than the torch, at any rate. The room was bigger than I thought.

"I can't believe this place." I moved away from the cupboards. "For a family that can't read, there sure are a hell of a lot of books."

Josh paused long enough to shove the torch into the pocket of his jacket then pulled the flat drawer out of one of the cabinets. "And maps."

A large book sitting on its own on a shelf caught my attention. It was open but sat upon a little stand, which kept the thick book mostly flat. I ran my fingers gently over the page, the film of grit from the fine layer of dust tickling my skin. I was pretty sure if someone who worked in a museum saw this book, they'd have a fit. Certainly, no environmental controls and white gloves here. The pages were thick and crinkled under my hand as I turned them.

"We also have a huge, whopping list of names."

Above me, there were several other thick books standing upright on the shelves. Those on the left had dates penned on pre-existing lines. Those on the right had blank lined spines.

"Here's 1823 to 1836. June 1836 to September 1842," I read out. The years were written as numbers; it was the cursive months that nearly tripped me up.

"Wow." Josh moved beside me and placed his hand lightly on the opposite page. "Of course, it's code. What does it say?"

"Tyrall, Drake John. Tyrall, Robert Brian. Tyrall, Bonnie Anne. July 4th, 1995. It's a record of some sort."

"What are the headings?"

"*Name, Pat, Mat, Birth, Death.*" I pointed to the top of the page at the column headings. "What do 'Pat' and 'Mat' mean?"

Josh shrugged. "Beats me. But 1995 is recent compared to the dates in the Chronicles. Hang on. I want to check something. Scoot back a bit. Check for Barbara Jasmine Borradaile."

I only had to flip back six pages. "Here we go. Borradaile, Barbara Jasmine. Borradaile, Montgomery Grant. Borradaile, Cornelia Isabelle. August 22 –"

"Dad and Mum." He clicked his fingers. "Paternal and Maternal. Father and mother."

"A record of ther... thop... shifters?"

"Could possibly be. Drake is the last entry in 1995, and Rachel did die that year." He flicked back again, running his finger down the names.

"You said you guys went back a long time. Where's the rest of the books?" I pointed. "There's 1805, but there's nothing earlier."

"Maybe they're somewhere else." He glanced around the room. "Or maybe that's as far back as the records go. Tasmania was colonised in 1803."

"What did they do before that?"

Josh shrugged. "Kept it in their heads. Cultures did that."

"Maybe the Elders would know."

"They might. One thing I do know, Uncle Scott would love to get his hands on these. I'm sure it would help with the—"

A long, shrill pip made us both jump. The pipping became shorter and more frequent.

"What the hell? Is that a telephone?" Josh moved sideways across the room with his head tilted.

I probably looked as strange as he did as we both tried to pinpoint the sound.

"I sure as hell didn't expect that." Josh pointed to the side of the cupboard. "Ginny, it's a security system, with a camera and everything."

There were four cameras. The black-and-white images came up in a quartered square on an old-style computer monitor with a chunky, large back to the screen. Three of the views showed three different angles of our driveway, and one showed the front of the house. It was a miracle it all still worked. As I watched, a familiar Land Rover drove down the driveway.

"Dad." I frowned. "He shouldn't be back this

early. We have to get back inside."

Flicking off the switch as he went past, Josh once again led the way in the dark. The long, dim corridor seemed even longer this time. An eternity passed as we hurried down the narrowing space, and I was sure Dad would find me missing and have time to completely flip out before we got back. My phone was on my desk. If he called it, I wouldn't be able to answer. Stumbling from the wardrobe, we dashed into the lounge room and barely had time to sit before I heard the car pull up out front.

Josh shoved all the papers messily into his satchel and yanked out my portfolio, which he promptly opened as he shoved his bag over his shoulder. At least one of us was thinking.

"Ginny?"

"In here."

"I forgot my work keys. Who owns the—" Dad appeared in the doorway between the kitchen and lounge room, holding the set of offending keys. "Hi, Josh. I assume that's your bike?"

"Yes, sir. I came to deliver Ginny's portfolio… again." He tapped the book. "I was about to leave."

"Good. Fine. I'll walk you out."

Josh handled the whole situation like he'd done this type of thing before. Acting like he'd only arrived, and wasn't covered in tell-tale silver cobweb strands. Dad didn't notice, which was just as well. I was struggling to come up with a plausible reason for the out-of-place arachnid homes. I was pretty sure I was going to get a lecture for having a boy in the house when Dad wasn't home, but it would obviously come tonight, because Dad was in a rush right now. Pretty soon, the sound of two engines trailed the two different vehicles down the driveway, and I was left alone.

I stood in the hallway for about three seconds before I made sure all the outer doors were locked, grabbed the torch, and headed back down into the room. I had a 'Lashed' beast to find, and a hell of a lot of Chronicles to read before I got there.

Chapter Eleven

"It's not an apprenticeship. Formal government apprenticeships don't exist. At least, not like a chef or a mechanic. But it's a job, if you want it."

I could nearly hear the wind whistle as it wound its way around the parked cars and skip bins that made up the space behind the Painted Serpent. Barbara hugged herself against the cold and looked down at the ground for a few seconds before taking a drag on her cigarette. I was shocked. When she rang last night for me to come to the Painted Serpent after school, I thought it would be about thylacine. Not a job. I hugged my zipped jacket around me, burying my freezing hands under my arms. If I was a smoker, standing in the freezing cold to be socially acceptable would put me right off the habit, cold turkey. Sad thing was, it didn't work for Barbara.

"What would I be doing, exactly?"

"General dogsbody stuff. Cleaning, ordering, and learning the computer system." She shrugged. "I do want to see what designs you can do. It'll be a casual job until we both feel this is where you should be. It's a hell of a risk, me taking you on. If you prove to be any good, you'll want to spread your little wings, and suddenly I've got competition. Not what I want in a small town."

"Then why are you taking the risk?"

"One, you do have some incredible talent, and I want to see what else you've got. And two…" She ground out the cigarette butt under her purple-glitter Doc Martins before bending to collect the butt and squishing it into the rusty tin hanging on the wall filled with others that had suffered the same fate. "The Elders have determined this would be an acceptable way for us to have contact with each other."

Until that very second, I'd been wishing like hell, she'd finish her cigarette fast so we could both go into the warm building. Now, I stood there like a stunned mullet as she opened the door. A part of me could see how the job could work as a plausible reason for secret thylacine business, but mostly I felt like she'd backhanded me with it.

"Well, aren't the Elders lucky I can draw?" I was pretty sure my tone was as bitter as the wind.

"And that you happened to walk into my shop looking for a job. Aren't they bloody lucky?"

Closing the door, I frowned at the way her tone nearly matched mine as she disappeared into the back room. "You don't want me to have the job?"

"To be honest, if they hadn't agreed to cover your wages, I would have turned them down flat. I built this business from scratch. I've already got Josh on board, and sure, an extra pair of hands would be welcome come event time, but on a day-to-day level, I don't need another person. If they want to pay you for reading a few coded books, then that's their worry."

Barbara stopped in the tea room and filled the jug with water.

"So, there isn't actually a job here?"

Turning with a sigh, she placed her hands on the sink behind her. "It's a small town, Ginny. There aren't many people who want art and piercings. And repeat business is months, sometimes years apart. General dogsbody, that's all I'm offering. The chance you'll work the gun is slim to none."

"Then what was with all the 'until we both feel this is where you should be' bull, if this isn't an actual job?"

"A good artist doesn't necessarily make a good tattooist. You have to be cut from a particular cloth for the job. It's got to be in your blood. If I think you've got that, then I'll start to train you. If I think you don't, then you've still got the job, because that's what the Elders want."

"And if I don't take the job?"

"Then we'll erase your memory and never have anything to do with you again."

"You can do that?" My voice squeaked.

She leaned forward and smiled. "No, but I thought you needed something to break the 'oh so serious' mood. Look, I may not need an extra person, but you have to admit it's a good deal. We all get a plausible time and place, and you get paid to be a Seer, and if we're both lucky, we'll get to learn something more about your drawing ability. Coffee? That's right. You drink tea, right?"

"Herbal, not black tea."

"Black, black, black, or coffee."

"I'm fine with hot water, topped with a touch of tap water."

Barbara made a face, but she made it along with her coffee and brought it over to the tiny, circular wooden table at the side of the room. As she stood, the buzzer from the front door of the shop went off.

"It's okay. It's only me," a male voice called out. Seconds later, a guy who didn't look much older than Barbara, with short dark hair and a navy-blue-and-brown padded jacket came around the corner. He was carrying a large cardboard file box. Halting a second, he stared at me before putting the box on the table. It took up nearly all the space.

"Hi, I'm Detective Scott Jeeter. You must be Ginny Martin."

I watched his thylacine check me out, and it took a second for his introduction and held out hand to register. "Detective?"

"Yeah." He reached into his pocket and pulled something out, handing it over to me. It was a gold badge, mostly circular with a crown on top of a star-burst kind of framing. A blue Tasmania shape sat in the centre, with a gold lion over the top of the state. I'd never seen a detective badge before. I had no idea if it was real or not.

"So, how do you fit into the picture?"

"I'm Cornelia's brother, and I'm investigating some murders I think you could help with."

I blinked. "Sorry? What now?"

Scott shucked his jacket, dragged the third chair across the room, and sat, placing one hand on the box as I handed him back his badge. "What I'm about to tell you doesn't leave this room, understood?"

I nodded.

"As I said before, I've been investigating some

murders. The latest being Victor Borradaile."

"Borradaile. A relation?" I crossed my arms.

"Cousin." Barbara told me. "His body was found just over a month ago near Cradle Mountain."

"The body the hikers found?" I winced as I realised that probably wasn't tactful of me.

"Yes." Her answer was rumbled low.

Scott didn't give me much time to feel awkward. He jumped right back in. "The murders happen about every three months, and their bodies are always found in the bush. The victims aren't the same, in age or gender, most are local, both newly local and generational, but one is a tourist, and I can't find a connection between them. At least, in the normal way of looking at them. I can only confirm three as therianthropes, but just because I can't confirm the others doesn't mean I don't think that's the connection."

"Okay." There was nothing like a nice, easy introduction into all this. He dumped it into my lap, and I was, somehow, supposed to catch all the pieces. I wasn't one hundred percent sure where this was going, but I was starting to think I might have an idea.

"As you can imagine, it's not a theory I can voice with my partner. Without confirmation, I can't start investigating it along those lines without raising questions. Josh thinks there could be a family connection between the victims, but not a direct one. He mentioned that a few weeks ago you saw a Silver attached to a woman he did not recognise as a direct family member, and that's what gave him the idea. I think it is extremely plausible. If the therianthrope link is confirmed, I can at least start to look further into family backgrounds and attempt to reasonably link them together that way."

"You can't start investigating family history anyway?"

"I've started, but I haven't got very far."

"You want me to look at stuff from your investigations, photos and things, to see if I can see a Silver and prove your theory."

"That's the idea, yes."

"Is this legal? Me looking at this stuff."

"I won't tell if you don't."

I glanced over at Barbara. She gave me a small smile and a shrug. "It's up to you. You don't have to help."

I nearly laughed. Both Barbara and Scott were acting all casual, but their thylacines went dead still, identical onyx stares drilling with laser intensity. It was almost like they were holding their breath, waiting for my next words, eyes boring into my brain. 'It was up to me,' my arse. I was pretty sure even if I said no right now, they'd find a way to point me back in the direction of helping them. "Since I'm here anyway, I might as well."

Their thylacines shifted again, and relaxed as if nothing in the world could ever bother them. I was still so conscious that they were watching me. It was weird. By watching the thylacine, I could almost tell exactly what the human counterpart was essentially feeling. That could be useful; I was sure of it.

"Josh says you can see the Silvers in video footage, so hopefully photos won't be different." Scott lifted the lid off the box. "I do need to warn you some of the images and details are graphic. Can you handle that?"

"I guess we'll find out." I'd seen crime shows

on TV. Hopefully, I could pretend the gruesome bits were stage makeup.

It nearly didn't work. The body in the first round of photographs had been torn to shreds. Bloodied scraps of skin peeled away like something had exploded it outward. Pieces of bone exposed. Yellow, green, maroon, and black were smeared around like globs of oil paint, with maggots and insects infesting the gory rainbow. I could almost see the movement in the still shots. Rushing filled my head, and I placed my hand on the table for a few moments, struggling to maintain my balance, until it passed.

"What could do something like this?" I pushed the photos away.

"My partner thinks this one was done by a wild animal."

"You think it's a thylacine?"

"If it is a therianthrope, it's being driven by its human side. Thylacines do kill animals—sheep, other marsupials, stray cats, things like that—but they're not vicious like this. Even in a Beast Walk, we naturally stay away from humans. That's why thylacines were considered shy."

"But what about other shifters? Devils and dingoes."

Scott handed me another file. "It's possible, but there's no way I can prove it."

"Why do you think there's a link in the first place?"

"The three-month timeline. Each of the victims in these files has the coroner's report placing time of death between the tenth and twelve of the month, February, May, August, and November, for six years."

"You think it's only one person killing them?"

"Could be a group. I don't know. This is why I need your help."

Scott put yet another file on my slowly growing pile. If he continued, the whole lot would end up on the floor. There wasn't much room left on the table; the box took most of it. Picking up the box, I put it on the floor next to him then moved the files over. Taking a measured breath, I reopened the folder and slowly searched the crime scene photos. I went through file after file, and after about nine, I shook my head. "Occasionally, I can see your thylacine in the photos, and sometimes two or three others in the background, plus the one I think belongs to your male ambulance driver with the red hair, but I can't see anything near the bodies. Maybe once the human counterpart is dead, they disappear."

"Damn it." Scott leaned back for a second. With a sigh, he shook his head. "Look, it's not your fault. Thanks for trying."

"Hang on." Barbara reached down to the open file on the table in front of me. "You can see Uncle Scott's Silver in the photo, right?"

"Yeah?"

"If you are right about the Silver disappearing when a therianthrope is dead, they should still show up in photos with them still alive, right? Do you have photos of the victims before they died? Like ones the family might have handed over or whatever?"

Scott reached across and flicked to the front of the file, the part I'd skipped because the photos of the crime scenes were further along, and showed the small photo attached to the page with all the common information on the victim. Name, address, date of birth, that kind of thing. The photo was only the head and shoulders of the woman with a blank blue background.

I shook my head. "I can't tell. I'd need more in the background."

"I don't have anything else." Closing the file, Scott collected it to put into the box, and as he did, a photo slid free. I picked it up. It was a full-length image of the woman, naked, on a steel table. She'd been cleaned up, and the white light glared off her skin but didn't obscure a silver glow emanating from the middle of her torso.

"Hold on one second."

"What?" Scott came closer.

"Lift your shirt?"

His head shot up. "What?"

"I think I see something, but I'm not sure. I want to see if I can see the same thing on you."

Without hesitating, he yanked up his shirt and jumper in one go, baring his body nearly up to his shoulders. He had the same silver glow in nearly the same spot as the photograph.

"Barbara?" I pointed to my solar plexus. "It's here. I don't need to see everything."

She pulled her shirt up too, not caring she flashed her bra and her awesome eagle tattoo. She had the same glow.

"Okay." I nodded. "I think this means she's a shifter. I can see a silver glow here, and you've both got the same thing."

"Here?" Scott pointed at his now clothed solar plexus.

"Yeah."

"That's where I feel the beast. The sense of it, I mean."

"Me, too." Barbara nodded.

Reaching across the table, Scott pulled the pile of previously searched files back in front of me.

He flicked through the top one for the autopsy photo. "What about this one?"

"Yes." I nodded. "Her, too."

I went through every single file. Fifteen women and ten men. It didn't matter if the skin was intact or not. Each one had a silver glow in the middle of their torso.

"Looks like you were right." Barbara told Scott as I closed the final folder. "Therianthrope is the connection."

"Now I have to prove it with a plausible finding."

"And connect it to the shifter or shifters responsible." I sat back in the chair.

Scott hesitated with a pile of folders in his hands. "I hope to God that it isn't a therianthrope."

"Because they don't kill people?" I wasn't being entirely sarcastic, but I was pretty sure the vibe was there.

"Because if one can deliberately murder while in a Beast Walk, then they are more dangerous than you can imagine."

"What if they are murderous in human form and then shift to kill?"

"Then that rules out thylacine. Anger's not a Beast Walk trigger." Barbara spoke as Scott placed the folders into the box.

"What about dingoes and devils?"

"Possible. They can shift whenever they want to."

"Proving all these people share a common ancestor isn't going to do much for your investigation, you know. It's too much of a stretch. I'm not so sure your partner will go for it."

Barbara passed a few files over to Scott. "She's right, you know."

"It's all I've got." Scott didn't look up from sorting files into boxes.

As I watched Scott pack up the files, I stared at the Tasmanian Police symbol on the front of the folders. The files were here, but we weren't set up in a police station.

"You're the only one looking into this, aren't you? This isn't an actual investigation. You're the only one who thinks the deaths are connected. You think someone is going after shifters?"

Scott nodded as he pushed the lid down on the box of files. "And you've confirmed it."

"If you can't provide evidence for it, it doesn't mean a thing, does it?"

"Not a whole lot, no."

"What the hell do you do now?"

"I need to know if someone is going after all therianthropes or just thylacines, but more importantly, how they know who to target. How long have you lived here?"

It took a second for the question to register. "Four months."

"And where were you before?"

"Townsville."

"Hang on. You think it's Ginny?" Barbara asked him. "Are you serious?"

"I thought it could have been a Seer… but…" Scott's tone was slightly defeated.

"But…?"

"But if you're the Seer… then it can't be, and I'm back to square one. Unless you've had someone working for you for the last seven years."

I frowned. "Why can't it be another Seer? And no, I didn't have anyone killing shifters for me. I didn't know they existed until about a month ago."

"The first-born granddaughter of the first-born granddaughter. There can't be two," Scott pointed out.

"Sure, there can." Barbara stood from the table. "If the grandmother is still alive when the granddaughter's born, then there are two."

"She died when I was two, remember? I don't think she's out there as a ghost, killing shifters."

"Unless you have a granddaughter."

"Seriously?" I stared at Scott, dumbfounded.

He shrugged.

"If you think about it, I might not be the only Seer, anyway. There could be three of us."

"Why three?" Scott asked.

"I'd never seen Silvers until I came here, and even though I've seen several thylacines, I haven't seen a Tasmanian devil or a dingo. Maybe there are Seers for each… you know, line or whatever, of shifters."

Both of them glanced at each other.

"What?" I asked slowly.

"Ginny, all lines of therianthropes do have their own Seers. And your theory is correct as far as I'm aware. They don't see Silvers from the other lines," Barbara told me.

Scott ran a hand through his hair with a shake of his head. "However, it still doesn't explain Victor, Rudolf Berringsly, or Hannah Ismay. Those three were confirmed thylacine therianthropes. If a Seer can only see a specific Silver, then the killer couldn't have seen their Silvers. Also, if it is the case, then all of them are thylacine therianthropes, because you could identify them."

"So, even though you now know they were all shifters, it opened more questions than it answered."

"That's about it."

"Glad I could help."

Chapter Twelve

"I'm not sure why you asked me to come here," Josh hissed nearly under his breath as we followed the woman in the pale blue shirt through the State Library of Tasmania.

"And you still came?" I frowned at him.

"Any excuse for a bike ride to Hobart."

"The only information I can find on the murder of Prudence Chesney is a possible article in the Tasmanian Mail, except when I clicked on it on the net, it said it hadn't been digitized yet and I needed to access it on the microfilm, here."

"So why am I here, exactly?"

I pointed a circular motion at my head. "Dyslexic. Small print. Doesn't normally mix."

"Why are we looking for her murder?"

"Thank you," I acknowledged as the library assistant pointed us to a huge cream-coloured machine with a large screen and two glass plates under it. She handed over five rolls of what looked like old film like they show sometimes in the movies. Before she went away, she used a sixth roll to show us how to use the machine.

"Those are the rolls for the Tasmanian Mail, 1910 to 1912. Let us know if you need any more."

"Sure, thanks." Josh smiled at her.

I waited for a few seconds until she was out of earshot before pulling the Chronicle I had nearly memorised out of my bag. "The Chronicles only go up to 1995. There's nothing that can help with the murders your uncle is working on, at least not until I figure out how to write the code and put it in there myself. However, and I know it's a long shot—I mean the murders are nearly a hundred years apart—but maybe there's something there. What if her murder wasn't random and it's somehow connected, maybe, perhaps." I shrugged.

"It's a thought." Josh sat in front of the machine and started moving the film. "Prudence Chesney."

Flipping open the red book, I double checked. "September 9, 1910."

Josh scrolled through for a long while. "Looks like it only came out weekly, and this one only goes until July. Can you pass the next one?"

He set the next one up and started scrolling through again. I had no idea how he could read that fast. The typed words would show on the screen for barely a second before Josh scrolled through a blur of black and white until he slowed it for the next second.

"Got it. Closest date is Saturday the 10th, 1910. Let's see what we can find here."

He scrolled through the film. This time, he didn't whiz through it, but carefully moved the images on the screen, section by section, reading for a few seconds before moving onto the next one.

From the outside, the library was a square box with windows. The inside wasn't much better. For a supposedly heritage listed building, it had a distinctive ambiance of a modern office. There was nothing architecturally interesting to look at, and there weren't enough visitors to "people watch" for long, either.

"Nothing."

"What?" I snapped my attention back to Josh.

"There's no mention of the murder."

"Impossible. Small town. Unsolved murder. There has to be something."

Josh whizzed the roll back to the start of that day's paper and carefully read every single headline and first paragraph aloud. It was interesting to hear how they worded things back then, but he was right. Absolutely no mention of a murder. For Prudence or anyone else.

I slumped back in my chair. "How is that possible?"

"She was a Seer. Maybe the Elders covered it up."

"Or…" I held up my hand. "They hadn't reported on it yet. Those articles, a lot of them started with 'last week,' 'late last Thursday,' or whatever. Maybe they didn't report things quite so fast back in the day. You said weekly, right? If the murder only occurred—"

"The day before the newspaper went out…"

Josh scrolled to the next edition and started reading the headlines. "*Double Mystery Murder of Locals*… Well, that's not… Shit."

"What?"

"*A tragedy at Queenstown on Friday last week, when Prudence Anna Chesney, aged 37, and*

Charity Wilson, aged 73, were found to be stabbed, nine and six times respectively." Josh frowned. "Who the hell is Charity Wilson?"

I moved closer, but the faded half type on the screen was impossible to read. "I don't know. Keep reading."

"*It is certain that both were murdered.*" Josh broke off and gave me a mock surprised look. "Really? You think?"

"It's a possibility." I tapped his arm. I wanted to him to continue reading.

"*Mrs Chesney was well known in the local community for petitioning and being instrumental in the successful ruling of the Tasmanian government to repeal the bounty law on Tasmanian tigers. It is suggested by some, that her activities in these matters might be a motivation toward the murders. However, police will not confirm this notion. Police investigations are underway. To date, no suspects have been declared.*"

I waited, but Josh didn't continue reading. "Is that it?"

"So far. Why didn't Rachel mention both murders in the Chronicle?"

I turned the book in question over in my hands, thinking. "It's for Seers. I suppose because Charity wasn't a Seer, maybe?"

"Could be."

I crossed my arms as I stared up at the not-quite-straight page on the screen. It had been scanned slightly crooked and the headline ran a little up screen like it had been frozen in some kind of escape attempt. "That doesn't tell you a real lot."

"It tells you somebody might be pissed off at her for getting the law changed about thylacines."

"Because… why? They wanted to keep killing thylacines?"

"Maybe they saw her predict the future and killed her for being a witch?"

I stared at him, attempting to send out the "seriously?" vibe. "That's comforting."

"It was 1910."

Crossing my arms, I sighed. "This was a waste of time, wasn't it?"

"Not completely." Josh started flying through the film again.

"You going to leave me hanging?"

"I'm checking three to four months either side."

"You think the three-month thing will be there too?"

"Don't know, but I'm not exactly a fan of all-consuming research, so we might as well get this over with today."

"Such positivity."

Three hours later and Josh had read practically every single headline, and the start of a fair few articles that showed promise. There were several deaths, and an attempted murder-suicide, where the intended murder victim survived but the suicide did not, listed in the rolls of microfilm we had, but nothing else that could possibly relate to murders approximately three months apart.

"Dead end," Josh announced.

"In more ways than one. Thanks for trying. I really thought it would lead somewhere."

"It's something you can cross off your list anyway."

"With nothing to replace it."

"So." Josh stacked the rolls of film into the small box they came in. "Do you want to spend what is left of the afternoon sampling the delights Hobart has to offer? The Museum and Art Gallery are a few blocks away, and they have a whole section on thylacine."

For a second, I was tempted. "I won't say no to something to eat, but I think we need to head off soon. It's four hours home, and the passenger seat of your bike is not the most comfortable place in the world."

Shaking his head, Josh laughed. "Pillion seat."

I picked up the box and shrugged. "Pot*a*to, pot*ah*to."

We handed over the box and walked out, heading for the reception counter where we had to collect our bags.

"So, takeaway or a full meal?" Josh pressed the button on the elevator.

"Probably takeaway. It's cheaper and less fuss."

"You are a cheap date, aren't you?"

"Even cheaper, because I'll be paying for mine, and when exactly did this become a date?"

Josh shrugged. "Figure of speech."

The elevator doors opened with an echoed ding. "Ginny? Hi."

Hopefully, I didn't come across as rude as I stood and blinked a few times before following Josh into the cubical. "Evie? It is a small world."

"I've just finished attending an event here. 'A Conversation with JF Penn,' an awesome thriller author. I can't believe I got to meet her, and I got a photo." Evie fisted her hands then held them up in a *stop* gesture. "I'll shut up now."

"That's okay. Something like that would be amazing."

"You have no idea. What are you doing here?"

"Helping me research an ancestor." Josh held out his hand. "I'm Josh, by the way."

"Evie Brawn. Nice to meet you. Did you find out much about your ancestor?"

"More than I knew before, but not as much as I wanted to."

As Josh and Evie carried on a conversation, I watched her very carefully. While she was all chatty and a little bit overly cheerful, her gaze kept flicking to the corner of the elevator. Down to where Josh's Silver was sitting. When the doors opened, Evie stepped out, turning back with a grin.

"See you Monday, Ginny. Nice meeting you, Josh."

"See ya." I gave a small wave then grabbed Josh's wrist to stop him from walking off. "Did you see that?"

"You mean the way she kept looking down into empty air, like you do?"

"Exactly. Just like me. Like she could see your thylacine."

"What do you know about her?"

"Not much, unfortunately."

"Maybe you need to know more." It wasn't a question.

"I'm sure I do."

The hours on the bike back to Queenstown were agonising. My backside had never been sorer. When you saw people riding on bikes, they looked like they were having the time of their lives. Maybe the driver seat was a cushy cloud. It had to be. The passenger seat was a thing snatched from a sadistic torture chamber. I was not a fan of motorbikes. At all. Never. Again.

The sun had been set for at least an hour by the time the house came into view, and I felt overwhelming relief I could now, finally, get off. The only thing that was kind of fun was holding Josh. He was all firm muscle and warm. And warm was needed when the open air whipped through the leather jacket.

The front light bathed the driveway in a golden glow, making ghosts of the trees and shadows of the early night. Josh held the bike steady with his feet as I swung off and removed my helmet.

"Thanks for tod—" A flashed streak of a large animal running at the edge of where the wash of light faded from the bush into the darkness at the side of the house caught my attention. "What was that?"

"A dog?"

"We don't own a dog."

Turning off the engine, Josh swung himself off the bike and removed his helmet. "Thylacine?"

"Then something would be wrong, right? Fight-or-flight response."

"Exactly," he said slowly.

Setting his helmet on the bike, he walked into the yard and around the house. I followed him.

"The backyard light is on," I pointed out.

"I can see that."

"It's a motion sensor. Something has to have triggered it."

"Hello?" Josh called out.

"Hey." Dad came out of the back shed, carrying an armful of wood. "You're home. Good. Dinner's about half an hour away. There's enough for three if you want something to eat, Josh."

"Thanks, but I should get home. Did you see

something just now?"

"Like what?"

"An animal of some kind. We thought we saw something."

Dad shrugged. "Probably a pademelon or something. I saw two earlier when I was mowing the lawn."

Both Josh and I pretended to accept that. There was nothing else we could do. If it was a thylacine, I certainly didn't want to bring unwanted attention to it. Pademelons were a smaller type of wallaby. They hopped. There was no way the animal we saw was hopping.

Chapter Thirteen

Josh tossed a kernel of popcorn into the air and caught it with his mouth. He was far too good at that. If I tried, I would have ended up covered in salt and butter, with popcorn bouncing all over the place. He hadn't missed a single one. I was happy with the coffee cup portion he'd filled for me from his bowl. I wasn't much into popcorn, but I'd taken it anyway. Josh at least attempted to treat me… I don't know, normally. Sure, we still had Chronicles and sketchbooks to go through, but the others made me feel like I should know everything by now. That they should all be able to shift at will in the ten days since finding the room under the house. Heck, it had taken Rachel years, and she had died without an answer. I'd only been involved in this stuff a little over two months. Josh tossed popcorn and attempted to get me to understand what was so awesome about basketball and his precious Hobart Chargers. The others shot quick-fire questions at me, like interrogating cops, and basically made me feel that spending time at school or sleeping was an inconvenient waste of time away from working on shifter stuff. Barbara was nice, but she was no exception.

"It doesn't look like you two are working very hard." She glanced pointedly at the pile of unopened books as she came into the tearoom.

"We are." Josh tossed another kernel, catching it with ease. "We're attempting to decipher hidden code."

"Hidden code?"

Reaching across, I passed the scrap of paper to Barbara. "I found this hidden in the back cover of the Chronicle. All it says is 'On the other hand.'"

"On the other hand? What does that mean?" Barbara handed back the scrap of paper and pinched a handful of popcorn from Josh.

"Don't know. But it must be important, otherwise it wouldn't have been in the back of the Chronicle."

"Are there more? In the back of the other books."

"Not in the ones I've read so far."

"How many are there?"

"About a hundred and fifty. I lost count."

Barbara choked on her popcorn. "Are you kidding me?"

I shook my head. "No. As far as I can tell, some Seers continued from the last Chronicle, and others started their own book, sometimes when another Seer was still writing in theirs."

Wiping his hand on his shirt, Josh pulled one of the other Chronicles closer to him.

"Careful, Josh, don't get icky stuff on that," Barbara told him.

"I wiped my hand." He wasn't too perturbed at

the scolding.

Tilting the book, he peered down at the page with a frown and his thylacine sat bolt upright.

"What is it?" I leaned forward.

"Just a second."

Reaching across, he grabbed a pen and a scrap of paper from the stationery tray behind him. Using his left hand, he wrote a few letters.

"Aren't you right-handed?" It was my turn to frown. The way he'd drawn the letters were rounded, shaky, and not all the letters were quite complete. I'd seen that before.

Josh looked up at me. "Do some of the Chronicles have writing like that?"

"Yes, how'd you…?"

"This is a Chronicle from the 1800s, right?"

"Yeah."

"The writing is printed, not cursive, and it seems slightly… uncomfortable. Like the author wasn't comfortable writing it, I mean."

"It's nowhere as bad as your effort." Barbara grinned.

"Yeah, but I haven't been writing Seer Code for most of my life either." Josh held the pen out to me, and his thylacine settled back down on the floor. It wasn't completely relaxed, but its ah-ha moment was over. It was just waiting now.

I pulled the paper closer and took the pen in my right hand. The way the pen sat on the paper felt kind of stiff, and it did not feel, in anyway, comfortable. As I wrote, I found my hand nearly flat on the page. That in itself felt wrong. I'd learned long ago to always write above the words; otherwise, I'd smudge the ink. Josh clapped with a laugh when I pulled away from the page.

"What?" I looked down at it, reading what I'd written. "'Josh is eating popcorn.' There's nothing too exciting about that."

Barbara pointed to the page. "It's in code, Ginny."

"It is?" I looked down again. Sure enough, once I focused on individual words, I could see the jumbled letters. I frowned at Josh. "How do you do that?"

"Do what?"

"You know what my predictions mean, and you figure out a cryptic clue in like, three seconds flat."

"I'm just that awesome." He laughed.

"Oh yeah, smarty pants." Barbara crossed her arms. "Who's the killer, then?"

"That one I'm still working on."

"Talking about killers, did you two get anything useful from your trip to Hobart?"

"Other than Josh needs a more comfortable seat on his bike if he's going to carry passengers?"

"Not much, no." This time, Josh ate a handful of popcorn like a regular person.

"But…" I held up a finger. "I've brought all the Chronicles I can find on Prudence. At least from the nearly sixteen piles of books I've searched so far. And I've brought all my sketchbooks so Josh can have a look-see. If I've ever drawn something even remotely relating to all this, I'm sure he'll find it."

"While you kids have fun with all that, I'm going to do some actual work. You know where the tea and coffee are, and Ginny, I bought a box of herbal tea for you. I think it's something like Strawberry Summer or some such thing."

"Thanks, Barbara."

I picked up a Chronicle I'd not read before. The

handwriting was new, it was dated 1829, and the Seer was writing about her new fiancé. My eyebrows lifted. Mostly the other Seers wrote about official Seer stuff. If I tried to read the records the Elders had, it probably wouldn't be much different. Usually. Mostly conflicts between shifters, family line things, the flare up of shifters being seen, and the hush-hush clean up afterward. Official stuff. This Seer used the Chronicle like her personal diary. And it made for some entertaining reading. Well, maybe entertaining wasn't the right word, but it was less dry than normal.

There was no sound between Josh and me, except for the occasional cough or sneeze for about two hours, so when he did eventually speak, I nearly jumped a mile.

"What's this?" Josh turned the book toward me.

I shrugged. "I don't know. I think it's a type of clock or something."

The drawing was of a circle of twelve different animals. A bee, cow, elephant, fish, grasshopper, horse, kangaroo, lizard, monkey, octopus, platypus, and a seahorse. Each of the animals had a cord tied around their middle, and each of the cords led to a sailing ship in the centre of the circle.

"You are so good at drawing. These look real."

"Thanks." I went back to reading.

"When did you draw this?"

"About Christmas last year."

"No, Ginny, look. This one."

He had moved on from the clock and was now showing me the gruesome dead girl.

"Um, about six or seven weeks ago, I guess."

Josh nearly ran from the room, taking the sketchpad and his hackle-raised thylacine with him.

I sat for about a second in shock before I got my butt into gear and followed him out into the shop. He was showing it to Barbara, whose thylacine was standing rock-still and staring at Josh. Without a word, she reached behind the counter and picked up the phone.

"Paul, it's Barbara. We need to get someone over to the Elliots' place right away. Ginny's drawn another picture. It looks like Anne Elliot could be the next victim."

"Wait." I crossed the empty shop to point at the sketchbook. "You know her? She's real?"

Josh nodded. "Second cousin… I think. Our mum and hers are cousins."

"Oh, shit."

This wasn't supposed to happen. She wasn't supposed to be real. She was supposed to be an actress in a late-night horror show. Not a person. Not truly dead. I stared at the page Josh still had open. It was surprising the grey graphite didn't turn red and drip from the page. Not another one. Please.

It was only when Josh waved his hand in front of my face I realised I'd missed the question.

"Huh?"

"Do your predictions always come true?" Barbara was still on the phone.

"Um… I don't know. Some do."

"She's not sure. Yeah, I know. Check out what the others think, but for my two cents, I'd say this is our best shot for catching this son of a bitch."

I hissed in a breath and barely contained myself until she was off the phone. "You can't use her as bait."

"We're not. But we are going to organise Elders to watch her, and when he comes for her—"

"Predicting the future isn't a science. Josh has more of a chance of figuring out how things work than I do. If you use her to catch him... her... the killer, it may be the one thing that gets her killed."

"Not if we can help it. And you said yourself predicting the future isn't an exact science. We could very well be saving her from the future you predicted. You did say only some of what you predict comes true."

"I said sometimes it comes true. I only know the stuff I experience or get told about. I've drawn lots of stuff I've never known if they've come true or not. If everything I draw does come true, then your actions could get her killed."

"And us not doing anything could get her killed, too."

"Damned if you do, and damned if you don't," Josh muttered.

"Exactly," Barbara told him. "But I'd much rather be doing something about it."

Chapter Fourteen

"So, what do you think?"

"Huh?"

My mind kept slipping off into part dread, part sickening anticipation, and part total hopelessness. It was impossible to know if acting on the prediction would save the girl or get her killed. I felt stuck on a downward spiral that wouldn't let me off. Anne Elliot. Having a name for her made it worse.

With difficulty, I brought my focus back to Evie and English class. Oh, right. Mr Goss had given us assignment sheets we were supposed to be looking at and choosing the topic of our next group assignment. If "group" could be used to classify two people.

I shrugged. "I don't know. I'm not all that into Shakespeare. I wouldn't have the foggiest which one to choose."

"Well, I love *Taming of the Shrew* so much I have it practically memorised. But I wonder if doing that one would be too easy? It would be more of a challenge to do one of the others."

"I don't mind easy."

Evie laughed. "You know most of the others will do *Romeo and Juliet*, don't you? It's the most well-known. We could do *The Tempest.* That's a fun one. *Midsummer's Night Dream* isn't on the list. Obviously too risqué for high school students. *Merchant of Venice*… hmmm, no. I don't like that one. The ending always feels rushed, like Shakespeare ran out of time when writing it and had to wrap it fast."

My eyebrows lifted. At least one of us would do well on this assignment. The only one I knew at all was *Romeo and Juliet*, and only because I had the Baz Luhrmann *Red Curtain Trilogy* at home.

"You did say you loved the *Shrew* one, so we could go with that." I gave a one-shoulder shrug.

"Okay, you twisted my arm. We could act out a scene as part of our oral presentation. This is going to be fun."

I stared down at the page. Act out? Not in my reality. Ever.

Evie laughed and patted my arm. "It's okay. You don't have to freak out so much. It was only an idea."

Tilting my head with a frown, I watched her circle *Taming of the Shrew* on the assignment sheet. Obviously, I wasn't as good at hiding my feelings as I thought I was.

"I'm assuming you don't really know *Taming of the Shrew?*" Evie was reading the instruction part of the assignment sheet already.

"Not much, no."

"And you're not a huge Shakespeare person?"

"That would be a slight understatement."

"That's okay. I've got several versions of it at

home, although I think the BBC *Retold* version might be more up your alley. It's always better to watch Shakespeare than to attempt reading it when you're a newbie."

"Okay. If you say so."

"What are you doing tomorrow night?"

"I'm not sure. I have a casual job and I don't always know if I'm working until that day."

"Well, I'll give you my number. If you're not working, we'll have a movie-study night."

Chapter Fifteen

"Shit, shit, shit."

Josh glanced at me as I buried my head in my arms, accidentally skidding the Chronicle I had dropped across the table toward him. I was pretty close to throwing it but only at the last minute stopped myself, so he was lucky. His thylacine didn't even lift its head at my outburst. Josh casually caught the blue soft-covered book one-handed before raising his eyebrows at me.

"That was eloquent."

"It's hopeless. There's nothing useful in here. Reading predictions decades old is next to useless. I need to go back seven years. What happened then? What trigged the murders? I have nothing. Nothing." I lifted my head. "And don't you dare tell me one of the predictions could lead us straight to the killer. There are too many of them. Look, hundreds of books, thousands of pages, and nothing to help narrow it down."

He didn't give me any reassurances that this wasn't a waste of time or try to convince me the

Elders thought it was important, or anything else I thought he would. He placed the Chronicle on the table, settled back in the chair, and turned the next page of my sketchbook.

"What do you want to do about that?"

His question surprised me.

"Do? There's nothing we can do."

"Okay, so we'll do nothing." He closed the sketchbook. "Want to come to the movies with me?"

"Huh?"

I sat up as he stood and started piling books on the table before slinging his satchel over his shoulders.

"It's Thursday night. Movies come out tonight. I'm sure there'll be something on."

"Are you kidding me?"

His thylacine got up and took two steps to the exit. I couldn't get my head around it.

"What? You. Me. Movies. It's not that hard. Your dad has the late shift. It's not like there's anything stopping you from going."

"But we've got...." I pointed at the unread Chronicles.

"Reading the Chronicles won't get you any closer to solving the murders, so why bother? Let's just chill, relax. Hang out."

I crossed my arms. "It's not just the murders, Josh. It's whatever this Lashing is."

"Oh, right." He nodded. "The Lashing."

My eyes narrowed as he leaned against the back of the chair. "What the hell is wrong with you?"

"Me? Nothing." The innocence in his tone was starting to rile me.

"Okay, what the hell is going on?"

"I'm going to the movies. Are you coming?"

"No, damn it." My confusion trickled over into anger and I glared at him. He was being an idiot. "Do you want to be able to shift at will, or not? There's more than the murders to solve here, and you know it."

"Yeah, I do." He tilted his head at me before removing the bag from over his head and sitting down. "Wasn't sure if you did."

"Of course I bloody well do."

"Then focus on that. Uncle Scott is dealing with the murders. That's not your job."

"No, I just draw the people who are going to die."

"You draw them, Ginny. You're in a position to see before it happens. You don't kill them. It's not your fault."

With that soft tone, he reached in and cracked something inside me. It shattered, the pieces shimmering in pale light before turning into dust and blowing away on the wind. There was no way he could possibly know. It had to be a lucky guess or a stab in the dark that hit way too close to home. He couldn't know. I stared up at his face. Into his eyes. He knew.

Damn it, he knew. Somehow, he knew I blamed myself for Shane's death. For the fact Anne Elliot was going to die. Stupid tears blurred my vision and I continued to stare at him, struggling to keep them at bay, not blinking, barely breathing.

Neither of us moved, caught in the echoed silence even the loudest shouting would never cause. It might have been better if he had yelled. I was pretty sure I could have handled that. It took a few more seconds of staring at him before I could finally breathe and blink away the tears, as if nothing had happened.

"Yeah, well what does it matter anyway? The predictions are stupid. What use is it that I predicted Mum would get Tina a bike for her birthday?"

His arms were on the table and he watched me for a few seconds. I nearly held my breath again. His eyes searched my face and I didn't look away. Finally, he blinked and I could breathe again.

"The same reason you drew a cool-looking clock, I guess. They may not be useful now, but something can still come of it."

"I hate all the unknowns and maybes. Could I for once, just once, have something clearly defined and easy to understand?"

"Nah." Josh leaned back and picked up the sketchbook again. "Where's the challenge? Don't want you getting too bored, now, do we?"

I glared at him for a moment longer, but he didn't notice. He pushed the Chronicle closer to me.

"There's something seriously wrong with you. You know that, don't you?"

"I do." A slow grin followed his cheerful words as he continued to ponder the sketchbook.

I waited, sure there would be something else. A lecture, maybe. Encouragement to talk about how I was feeling. Warnings about not bottling stuff up. There wasn't. But it was still a long time before I could stop staring down at the page and start reading the coded words again.

Chapter Sixteen

"G'day. You must be Ginny."

"Hi."

"I'm Yolanda, Evie's mum. Come on in. She's setting up in the lounge room."

The house was wonderfully warm, and as I stripped off my jacket, bright yellows and blue highlights caught my attention. Pieces of driftwood, baskets of shells, displays of broken glass bottle shards arranged in mosaics, and splashes of bright, bold colour were everywhere. It was amazing. In a cold, gloomy Tasmanian autumn, their house was like a little seaside cottage. Everything was bright, airy, and colourful. Mismatched DIY recycled furniture filled in the spaces, tied together only with the colour theme, which ran around the house in a rainbow. It was so different to the dark, almost sombre emptiness of home. Nothing matched. Everything pulled your attention from one item to the next. It was fantastic. I fell in love with the place instantly.

From pale lemon to an almost orange-gold, the

colour yellow united the lounge room. The painted frame of the mirror, the table runner on the coffee table made of tied strips of old yellow plastic bags, yellow cushions, and the yellow painted driftwood from which hung decorated egg shells I assumed were left over from Easter. All that tied together the two wooden armchairs, the wicker-framed couch, the coffee table made from an old tree stump, and the TV and electronics set up in Meccano-styled tin shelves. As a decorating scheme, it shouldn't have worked, but it did.

"Yay! You're here." Evie stood from where she'd been kneeling in front of the TV. "Grandma's made some popcorn and chocolate chip biscuits for us. You're not allergic to anything or on a diet, are you?"

"No."

"Great. Because her chocolate chip biscuits are to die for. She'll bring them out when they're ready. I'll grab my books."

Curious to see a little more of the house, I followed her. Her room was all shades of green, down to the wood and rope shelves holding dozens and dozens of green glass bottles of all shapes and sizes.

"Are there really ninety-nine up there?" I pointed.

"Ha, ha. No. Only seventy-three, but I'm working on it."

She went to her desk. Above it was a yearly calendar, next to a monthly calendar on a white board with numbers up to thirty-one and a space to write the month. My name was written in the square with today's date, but the other dates had Biology, Math, Chemistry, Physics and other stuff written on it.

"What's that?"

Evie glanced up at it. "My homework calendar."

"Far out, you're organized. Do you really take three science classes?"

"Yep. I want to be a vet. That's why I need to do well in English, too."

"And you got stuck with me. Sorry."

"That's rich coming from Miss 'I got a B+.'"

"Yeah, my first ever."

"Well, stick with me, do your share of the work, and we'll get you your first A ever."

I snorted as I followed her back to the lounge room, the popcorn and food already on the coffee table. "Good luck."

She started the movie. "Now this one I'm showing you is the *Shakespeare Retold* version. They speak modern English most of the time."

"Good to hear."

About two hours later, I blinked owlishly when Evie turned the light back on.

"What did you think?"

"I think he's crazy and they're both as bad as each other."

Evie laughed. "Uh huh. So, what do you reckon? One of the themes should be 'crazy attracts crazy'?"

"Very funny. I think he had to be crazy to 'Tame the bitch.'" I used air quotes with my fingers, because that's what the male character, whose name I'd forgotten, had said in the movie. "I mean, everyone else tried to calm her down using reason and pleading, and she exploded every time. He was crazy, illogical, and sometimes just plain weird, but every time she lost her temper, he got weirder. When she was pleasant, he was nice."

Evie grinned and reached for an exercise book. "And you thought you weren't any good at this."

"Girls, do you want something to eat?" a new voice called from somewhere else in the house.

"Food." Evie jumped to her feet. "Coming, Grandma."

She led me to the kitchen. It was an open plan kitchen-dining room, but the kitchen accents were purple and the dining room was orange. It moved seamlessly, one into the other, without missing a beat. I couldn't believe this crazy decor thing worked.

I was expecting more chocolate chip biscuits and maybe a drink, not a full meal. Evie's grandma was dishing up lasagne and salad. She wasn't the typical soft and cuddly fluffy-haired grandma. Her grey hair was straight down her back and she wore loose clothing in bold patterns with a ton of bright jewellery.

"Wow, thanks, Grandma." I didn't have another name for her.

"Can't have you girls studying on an empty stomach, now can we? My name's Miriam, by the way." She held out a loaded plate for me.

As I took it from her and turned toward the table, Evie stiffened, her voice coming out like she was in a trance. "The one who is, is not who is thought, and can yet be saved through loss."

What held me captive wasn't her words, but the fact her eyes changed to bright, deep purple.

Evie shook her head and blinked, her eyes rapidly returning to green.

"She's epileptic. She sometimes has fits."

Yolanda hurriedly crossed to the table and placed a hand on Evie's arm. "Are you okay?"

For a second, I wasn't sure if she thought that was true or if it was an agreed story for outsiders, until Yolanda handed Evie a small, apparently well-used notebook and pen.

I turned to Miriam. "I suppose you're epileptic like Evie."

Miriam tilted her head with a quizzical glance. "Yes, it runs in the family."

"Skipping a generation."

She opened her mouth to answer then frowned as she stared at me. In fact, I had everyone's attention.

"Why do you say that?" Yolanda asked.

"Purple eyes and the habit of looking at something that doesn't appear to be there for anyone else. I'm assuming 'epileptic' is your code for 'Seer.'"

"Well…" Now Miriam's gaze went from quizzical to wide-eyed surprise. "That's a first."

"See, Mum, I told you she'd know. As soon as I—"

"But how is this possible? It runs in a family line. And there is already a Seer." I didn't mean to interrupt Evie, but I couldn't help it. "Sorry."

"For the canis lupus? That's not possible." Miriam sat at the table.

"Hang on, wait." I held up my hands. "You're the Seers for… dingoes?"

"Yes, who did you think we were?"

"Thylacine. That's why I was confused. And isn't it canis lupus dingo?"

"You don't need the 'dingo' bit, it's superfluous. And there isn't a Seer for the

159

thylacine." Evie grabbed two of the plates of food and set them on the table, placing one in front of Miriam and sitting herself in front of one.

"Why do you think there isn't one?" I sat down with my plate of food.

"Their Seer died years ago." Miriam accepted utensils from Yolanda, who also sat with her food. The way they did things was almost like a TV family, all flowing, rehearsed motions. "All records indicate her family line died out."

"Which doesn't make life any easier for us." Evie spoke around a mouthful of food.

"Why is that?"

"Do you know about the murders?" Yolanda asked.

I lowered my fork. "You know about that?"

"That's why we're here. Mum and Evie started to have predictions relating to the murders several years ago."

"How'd you know the murder victims were thylacines?"

Yolanda waved her fork in Evie's direction before using the utensil to mush up her lasagne into her salad. "The first few of Evie's predictions relating to this said thylacine. We've been trying to get in contact with the thylacine therianthropes ever since, and you can't exactly put out an ad in the newspaper. By tradition, we would need an introduction by the Seer to the therianthropes, which makes things harder also."

I smiled. "I reckon an ad could work. Those that know would understand. And those who don't wouldn't."

"Tasmania isn't like the rest of Australia. Back in the 1800s, the Government found out about the therianthropes and put a bounty on thylacine, trying to eradicate them. You never know who has long memories around here. We announce our presence and the wrong people find out we're attempting to stop the murder of therianthropes, it could be devastating for us."

Stunned by Yolanda's revelation, I slumped in my chair with my hand at my mouth. The Government knew? Suddenly, Prudence's death got a whole lot more sinister.

"You're… um…" I cleared my throat and tried again. "For a family trying not to inform the wrong people, why do you trust me enough to tell me?"

"Well, duh." Evie laughed. "You're a canis lupus therianthrope."

My fork made a loud clatter as it tumbled from my fingers. "I'm sorry? What?"

They shared confused looks.

"You're a canis lupus therianthrope." Miriam pointed toward the kitchen counter. "Your Silver is right there."

"You didn't know?" Evie frowned. "How is that possible?"

"If you didn't know, then how do you know about therianthropes in the first place?" Miriam asked.

"Because I'm the thylacine Seer."

Chapter Seventeen

"You're a therianthrope?" Josh pulled himself up onto the steel table next to me.

"Apparently."

I didn't look up. If I ignored him, maybe he would go away. I didn't need this right now. The Borradailes' attic looked like Murder Mystery Incorporated. A huge board was set up with notes, photographs, maps, and theories. Boxes, files, and papers were everywhere. I was pretty sure Scott was excited about getting two new fresh sets of eyes and a whole heap of potential new evidence to help. It took all of twenty minutes after the introductions for us all to be dragged up here. About an hour after that, the rest of the thylacine Elders arrived. There was quite a crowd at the other end of the room. Seven in total, not including myself. The Brawns, the Borradailes, and the Elders swarmed over everything. An interesting pattern was forming on the map based around Cradle Mountain as they worked.

"That is awesome." Josh grinned. "And the best

part is you can Beast Walk whenever you want."

Ignoring him wasn't working. Begrudgingly, I brought my attention back to him and his stupid grin.

"I don't think so."

"You don't think that's the best part?"

"I don't think I can Beast Walk. I never have before. And I don't feel a ceast anywhere here." I circled my hand in front of my chest.

"Maybe canis lupus feel it somewhere different."

"Maybe." I looked back down at the photographs I'd been asked to go through. It wasn't a real task. I wasn't looking for anything in particular. Just being a different set of eyes might pick up something other people hadn't noticed. Maybe if I stared at the photo long enough, he would realise I was busy. Very busy.

"Oh, maybe." Josh slumped as he mimicked an old, grumpy, sad sack. "Maybe... nothing. Aren't you even a little bit excited?"

"No, Josh." I glared at him. "I'm not excited or special. I'm just a girl who, until a few months ago, thought being dyslexic was as far from normal as I could get. And now I wish it was."

"Well, I suppose it could be considered a shock to the system."

"You think?" I stared up at him in mock surprise for a second before I shot him a glare and went back to the photos.

"I could teach you to Beast Walk, you know. It can't be much different."

I didn't look up. It took everything I had not to scream at him. Did he not see I didn't want to talk about it?

"Canis lupus don't need flight-or-fight, so what could you possibly teach me?"

Josh was silent for a while as I flipped through the images, and the sight of his legs swinging out of the corner of my eye was starting to annoy me.

"One of your parents has to be a therianthrope, you know."

"Oh, for Pete's sake. Drop it, will you? I don't want to do this."

I slammed the photos down between us and stalked off. Exiting the attic, I nearly ran down the two flights of stairs into the kitchen. I felt trapped. Dizziness was crowding my head. This house. The shifters. Their world. It was all around me and there was nothing that would stop it from dragging me under. The only reason I was here, the only reason I connected the Brawns to the Borradailes, was to stop the murders. To keep Anne Elliot alive. That was it. When it was over, I was done. When this was over, they could all go crawling back into their own supernatural darkness for all I cared.

Flinging open the front door, I came to an abrupt stop on the wide cement stairs. I had nowhere to go. Cornelia had driven me out here, and I couldn't very well go stomping off into the bush that was their property. Dusk was greying the sky and lengthening all shadows into darkness. I was pissed off, not stupid.

I allowed my knees to buckle and dropped down on the stone stairs leading out into their front yard. The cement still held some heat from the day. I wasn't sure how long it would last, but for now, it meant I wasn't freezing. At least not yet. I was pretty sure it wouldn't be long in coming though.

Leaning my head against the wall of the

balustrade, I closed my eyes. I was so close to losing it again. It was pathetic. I wasn't someone who cried, but I came close far too many times around these people. It needed to stop. Tears nearly fell, and I screwed my eyes shut so hard I could see golden rings.

I couldn't let them find out how freaked out I was. Not only was I Seer; I was a damn shifter. A being who transformed into an animal. It wasn't possible. It wasn't right. A Seer... I could handle that. It explained my Drawing images, it helped explain a lot of unanswered whys. The shifter thing, that was too far. Normal hadn't merely slipped through my fingers. It had been run out of town on a rail, tarred and feathered, banished, never to return. I was drowning. And Josh, the one person I thought I could count on, the one person who'd helped me find my feet in all this, was the one who was now pushing me into the abyss. I had drawn my boundary lines to keep myself intact, and I couldn't, I wouldn't, step over that line. If I did, everything would fall apart. There would be nothing left of me, and I wasn't about to disappear. There was no way I was reaching that place. Ever again. I didn't need another shrink telling me how to pick up the shattered pieces.

My heartbeat was frantic, and I deliberately slowed my breathing. Calming down. Breathe in, breathe out. One breath at a time. One heartbeat at a time. Now that the thudding through my body was easing, I could focus on the quiet hush around me. I could feel the walls melting away. It was so quiet out here. At my house, Dad always had the TV or radio on. Some background human element. Right now, I couldn't hear anyone in the house, and all around me the chorus of birds sung, saying goodnight. The tension eased like a blown puff of dandelion fluff.

The bush had its own unique scent. It was damp and earthy, new growth and decay. I had to admit the scent of the bush was one of the things I loved about Tasmania. Sure, you didn't have to go far out of Townsville for bush either, but it smelled different. Back home, it smelled dusty, hot, and wide open. Here, it was… comforting.

"Peace offering."

With a gasp, I jumped at the sound of Josh's voice. Looking up at him, I stared at the steaming mug he offered. If I didn't take it, would it mean he'd go away? No such luck. He took a few steps down, stood for a second, and then sat on the step one above me, his Silver curling up between us. With a sigh, I held out my hand and took the mug of tea. I didn't want the drink, but I was thankful for its warmth against my fingers.

"I can understand how freaked out you must be. You've had a totally new world shoved on you over the last two months, and now this."

I didn't comment. Resting my arm on the cement railing, I stared out into the trees that were nearly all shadows under the navy sky.

"You're not the only one tripping out. I think the Elders are in a tailspin. Our Seer is a canis lupus."

"Is that supposed to make me feel better?"

"I guess not." He took a mouthful of drink and stared into his own mug. "It's not something to be scared of, you know. It's like… bungee jumping. There's the slight resistance just before you cross over, and then it's… exhilarating. Exciting.

Freedom. All restrictions fade away."

"I don't like bungee jumping."

"Have you ever tried?"

"No. But I've been on a roller coaster, and I hated it. So I don't want to go anywhere near jumping on a giant elastic band. I don't even like it when the car goes over a hill too fast. I hate that sensation of your tummy getting left behind. I have to figure out how to Unlash your beasts. We're running out of time before the next murder. I still have school and homework... and now this. Can't I, please, finish one thing at a time?"

I could feel everything rising up in a wave to drown me, and held my breath.

"Stop the world. I want to get off," Josh muttered.

"Exactly." The word came out on a rush of air when he didn't push.

"Well, since we've got a thousand people working on the murders, where are you up to with the whips and lashes?"

It took a second to realise he was teasing me and I smacked his leg. "Don't be such a dag."

"What can I say? Sticks and stones may break my bones, but whips and chains excite me."

"You are such an idiot."

"Would you look at that, ladies and gentlemen? A genuine smile. And the crowd goes wild." He shook his clasped hands in the air in a victory move and made mock cheering sounds before calming down. "Seriously though, where are you up to with that?"

"Nowhere. I did find out Charity is... was Prudence's mother." I sighed. "I don't really know, Josh. There's so much information, and most of it bears no relation to what I want to find out. I think Lashing is something done deliberately, because Prudence writes *'it is time to undo what has been done.'* My theory is Prudence Lashed the beast to protect the shifters from total annihilation, but was murdered before she could finish unlashing them. I just don't know how."

"So, we can't Beast Walk, because we were being protected? That's a new one."

"Have you got a better idea?"

He held up his hand. "It makes sense. I never thought of it like that before."

"What? Did you think it was a punishment or something?"

"Yeah, actually." He picked his mug up from the step and took a mouthful. "Do you reckon there's something in your dungeon that will tell you?"

"What is up with you? Whips, chains, and now dungeons. Are you some kind of masochist or something?"

"Whip me, beat me, tie me up," he teased.

With a slow smile, I leaned in close to him. "No."

He stared at me in shock, and then burst out laughing. "You're a closet sadist. Who knew?"

I gave him a shove with my hand, and the next thing I knew, my hand tingled, and Josh had disappeared. I was pushing against a thylacine.

"What the hell?" I scrambled to my feet, only dimly aware of the sound of breaking glass as my mug tumbled from my lap, and I stared at the blurry beast on the stone steps. Josh was crouching as a Silver between us. I spun, my heart racing as I searched for whatever it was to cause Josh to shift. I couldn't see anything. Slowly, I turned back. The thylacine was still there, and if an animal could look shocked, I'd say that was what it was doing.

Josh's human Silver made some motions with his hands. First, he waggled his finger from side to side then ducked one hand under the other. He didn't mouth any words, but I understood what he was asking, because it was the same question I had.

"I don't know," I told him. "I have no idea what happened, but one thing's for sure. You've Beast Walked without flight or fight."

Josh's Silver was ecstatic and within seconds, both of them, the Silver and the thylacine, had disappeared into the shadowed bush. I was left standing there, staring into the darkness. I had no idea thylacines could move so fast. It was nearly impossible the Silver would be able to keep up. Obviously, it could.

Bending down, I collected the three broken pieces of my mug and Josh's half full one. I left his clothes where they were, but I did fold them. Somehow, I didn't think he'd be back in a hurry, but he'd need them when he did. I went back inside.

Barbara leaned against the table next to me after I returned to the attic and resumed looking at the photos.

"Have you two made up now?"

Far out, obviously it was too much to ask to be able to go through the photos in peace.
"Apparently."

"Where is Josh, anyway? We need him to take you home before your father shows up at the parlour looking for you."

"Went for a Beast Walk."

"What?" Her lounging posture snapped into an

upright one. "What happened?"

"Not sure. One second, he was Josh, and the next, he was a thylacine."

Barbara sighed and ran a hand through her hair. "All right. Where'd you put his clothes?"

"On the front steps."

She didn't answer. Instead, she went over to the others and told them what happened. The thylacine Elders, all six of them, just about went into cardiac arrest and came at me like a flock of seagulls over a chip.

"What happened?"

"Is anyone hurt?"

I backed up against the wall. "Nothing. No one."

"Ginny, please tell us what happened. It's important." Cornelia placed her hand on my shoulder.

"I don't know. He was Josh, and then he was a thylacine."

"Did you touch him?" Miriam asked calmly from the other side of the crowd.

"Yeah, I kind of pushed him."

"And your hand moved from him to his Silver?"

It took me a second to run the memory through my mind. "Yes."

"I wouldn't worry about it. Sounds like Ginny merely forced a walk on him."

"I'm sorry? Forced a walk?" That was the old guy whose face was so lined it looked like scrunched paper. Aside from the Borradailes and Scott, I hadn't been introduced to the other two Elders, so I didn't know his name.

"Yes, the same as you do when you're teaching

children to Beast Walk."

Evie's gasp made me jump. "Except you haven't had a Seer for like, fifteen years, so you wouldn't know what a forced walk was, would you?"

I thought about correcting Evie about when Rachel had died, but it wasn't important right now.

Miriam frowned and gestured to the guy with the scrunched paper face. "Of course they would. Paul would certainly know."

"He might, but I don't." I didn't care if I was pushing my way into the little exclusive club or not. I had a right to know what the hell was going on.

"A forced walk is where a Seer uses the Funem-vitea to transition a therianthrope into or out of a Beast Walk," Miriam explained.

"And what's a 'funky vita-brick' when it's at home?" I crossed my arms.

Evie laughed. "Funem-vitea. The thread that connects between the body and the Silver."

"What thread?"

"The glowing strand thingy that goes between them." She moved her hand back and forth as though between two invisible items.

I shook my head. "There is no thread."

"No thread?" Slowly, Miriam stood. "That may explain why thylacine cannot Beast Walk at will. The Funem-vitea contains the force... the essence that creates the transition for therianthropes. Without it, there can be no transition."

"We can still Beast Walk when the need arises," Cornelia reminded her.

"Have you ever heard of 'Lashing the beast'?" I nearly held my breath, and several heads snapped towards Miriam, waiting for her answer.

Miriam shook her head. "No. What is it?"

Shrugging, I tried to play it down. "Something I read. I thought it might be something."

Barbara held up a hand. "Can we go back to the part where the Seer can make a therianthrope Beast Walk? Are you seriously saying Ginny can cause any one of us to Beast Walk, like, right now if she wanted to?"

"A canis lupus Seer can. I assume it would be the same for thylacines."

"Can she do it now?"

I looked at Barbara in surprise. There was pure excitement on her face, and she seemed dead keen. In fact, every thylacine Silver in the room nearly quivered in what I could only describe as anticipation.

Miriam ran a hand over her mouth. "I suppose I could attempt to instruct her. It might be easier if I force a walk on you, Ginny—"

"Hell no. That ain't happening." Dread nearly made me dizzy again and I held my hands up, taking a giant step back even though there was a table between us.

"I wouldn't leave you as a dingo. I would transition you back directly."

"Not a chance."

"Just walk her through it, Grandma. It might be called a forced walk, but doing it against her will isn't going to help anyone."

"I don't intend to do it against her will."

"You said there was no Funem-vitea, right?" Evie asked.

I glanced between them carefully. They stayed on their side of the table, and for now the threat of forcing a walk was over. Slowly, I nodded. "Right."

"Can you see anything on the body that might indicate where it would be attached? I mean, they have Silvers, so they have to be connected somehow, even if you can't see it."

"What kind of anything?"

Evie tapped her stomach. "Canis lupus have the Funem-vitea connected at their belly buttons."

"Sarcophilus harrisii connect at the small of their backs," Miriam added.

"Would the connection glow?"

Miriam and Evie looked at each other then spoke in unison. "Yes."

"Solar plexus." This time, it was Barbara and Scott who spoke together.

I shrugged. "What they said."

"Imagine, if you will, a plank of wood. At one end of the wood is a hole." Miriam walked around the table, and it took every thought process not to back away from her. "Through this hole is a piece of rope. At each end of the rope is a wooden ball, one painted green and one painted blue. Now imagine the rope is pulled all the way through the wood until the green ball is against the plank, the blue is dangling all the way down the other end. Are you seeing that in your head?"

"Yeah."

"In this position, the green end represents the human form and the blue end represents beast form. The plank represents what is currently the flesh and blood body. Do you understand so far?"

"Yes."

"In essence, what you need to do is move the plank along the rope until the blue end is against the plank."

"And the beast becomes the flesh and blood," I

guessed.

Miriam nodded. "Yes. That is how it works. I don't know how this will happen without a Funem-vitea, but we're about to find that out. Who would like to be Ginny's guinea pig?"

"It would make sense if I was. I have a pretty good idea where Josh would have gone." Barbara's tone was calm, but her thylacine was practically shaking.

The other thylacines were not happy with that. One of them went all hackle-raised and everything. I held up my hands before a huge argument could break out.

"I'm sure I'm going to need a few goes at this. What if I tried with Barbara first, and then I could do each of you. You all get a chance to Beast Walk if you want to, and we have a better chance of finding Josh. Then I can get home before it gets too late and my dad starts to get all parental. Deal?"

"That sounds sensible." Paul nodded. "Miriam, if you would continue."

I sighed. At least the thylacines all calmed down. The human counterparts might have been adult and rational about it, but they were probably about to go as ballistic as their beasts. I might not want to explore the world as an animal, but it was pretty unmistakable that they did. And it wasn't something they could do very often.

"When you touch your hand to the flesh, at the connection of the Funem-vitea, your hand becomes the plank in my imagery. You need to move your hand to the Silver, moving from the green end to the blue. Once your hand touches the connection of the Funem-vitea of the Silver, the Silver will transition into flesh, and the human into the Silver.

My eyebrows lifted in surprise. "As easy as that?"

Miriam nodded. "As easy as that."

"I thought it would be more complicated."

"Perhaps with thylacines, it will be."

And like that, I was pulled further into their world. Half of me wanted to run screaming from the room. The other half of me desperately wanted to make this work. If I could get this to work, then they wouldn't need me for much longer. I was so backward and forward at the moment I wasn't sure I knew which way was up. There was nothing for it. I couldn't stay undecided forever. I walked closer to Barbara and hesitantly placed my hand at her torso. There was nothing to be worried about. I'd done this to Josh by accident, so doing this on purpose shouldn't be any different. Telling myself that, didn't lessen the tightening knot in my stomach.

"You'll be fine," Evie spoke quietly.

I was sure I came across pretty calm, and it made me wonder what my Silver was doing for her to say that. Quickly, I squashed that thought. I didn't want to know anything about my Silver. It could cease to exist as far as I was concerned. Right now, I needed to focus on Barbara. Other than her body through her tattooed Snow White T-shirt, I didn't sense anything. There was no tingle, no extra warmth, no other-worldly sensation. Nothing to indicate I was anywhere near the thread thing. With a sigh, I dropped my hand.

"Whoa." When I pulled my hand away, I felt tingles and my palm was glowing. I'd felt the tingles with Josh, but the glowing was new. "Can you see that?"

Barbara looked at my hand, which I was slowly

rotating, checking out the glow from all angles. "See what?"

"My hand is glowing."

"Not your hand." Miriam stood next to me. "The Funem-vitea. You have hold of it."

My palm was open and I couldn't tell I held anything. Crouching down, I passed my hand through Barbara's Silver. As soon as my hand cleared it, the Silver became Barbara, and a live thylacine was standing where she had been.

"It worked." The gasp came from the female Elder I still didn't know the name of.

"Of course it worked," Miriam told her. "Ginny is a Seer."

I took a reactive step back and stumbled as I was mobbed. Five voices all talking over the top of each other was a lot to handle. Even Miriam and Evie had to cover their ears.

"Wait. Back up. Cornelia, you're next. Yours is the only Silver I recognise. The rest of you... other side of the room, now." I pointed. "I don't know which Silver belongs to who, and because I'm pretty sure it won't work if it's the wrong Silver, you can all bloody well wait your turn."

"I cannot believe Ginny has to tell you that. Even children know how to wait in line."

I was pretty sure the Elders didn't appreciate Miriam's input, but I was more than a little relieved to have someone on my side after I'd roused on a group of adults.

Cornelia was next, then Monty, Scott, Paul, and the female Elder, whose name I found out was Lexie. It was surreal to be standing in a room surrounded by thylacines. The human Silvers had already left the attic.

"That's so flipping weird."

I turned toward Evie. There were too many "weirds" at the moment to identify exactly what she meant. "What is?"

She pointed to the piles of clothes on the floor. "That. They apparently can't Beast Walk with their clothes."

"And that's weird?"

"Well, it doesn't happen with canis lupus. That's for sure."

I looked down at the clothes, not knowing what it meant, if anything, and realised the thylacines were all still crowding the room. "Well, what are you waiting for? Go find Josh."

"Ginny." Miriam held up her hand.

"What?"

"They're thylacines. They can't open the door."

Chapter Eighteen

Finally, I was getting some drawing done. Of my own. Not a prediction. And not related to shifters. Barbara had given me the task of coming up with a design. A woman with a mastectomy scar wanted an underwater scene with a seahorse included to cover what was left of her breast. I had a black-and-white representation of the size and shape of the scar, and that was it. I was surprised Barbara had given me something like this off the bat. I expected something small, like a butterfly or a single flower. I was half convinced this wouldn't turn into a tattoo; it was a test with no real payoff, but I was going to do the best job I could. I was determined to prove myself useful without all the Seer entanglement. This was going to become a real job, whether she wanted it to or not.

The door chime sounded, and I looked up from the aquarium reference book I was studying.

"Miriam, hi."

She wasn't alone. She was with another woman who was about Cornelia's age and had a long, thick grey plait tossed over her shoulder.

"Hi, Ginny. Is there somewhere we can talk?"

My eyebrows lifted at the seriousness of Miriam's tone. "Sure, I'll let Barbara know we'll be out back."

There was only one customer, and Barbara had been working on his bicep for about forty minutes already. I didn't think she'd miss me for a few minutes. I led the two of them into the staff room. "What's up?"

"Ginny, this is Lori Witters. She's the sarcophilus harrisii Seer."

I frowned for a second before comprehension dawned. The Tasmanian devil. "Wow. I hadn't expected that."

"Yes, well when Miriam told me the thylacines had a Seer, you could have knocked me down with a feather, so I suppose that makes us even." Lori pulled a tablet out of her bag. "I need to show you something. It'll help you understand."

I didn't know what to expect, but it certainly wasn't photographs of Tasmanian devils with deformed and disfigured faces. Twisted white lumps of skin pushed out of their fur. Red and weeping wounds crusted with black scabs. Mouths and noses so distorted and twisted I couldn't see where the facial features were.

"Devil facial tumour disease or DFTD," Lori explained as she swished the screen to the next photo. "The first official case of it was registered in 1996, but we first saw it emerge two years earlier. We didn't know what it was at the time. We now know it is a parasitic cancer. I won't bore you with details, but the same genes that are in the tumour cells are also in the sarcophilus harrisii immune systems. When the therianthropes Beast Walk, their immune systems don't recognise the tumour cells as foreign. The cancer does not distinguish between therianthropes and origin devils."

"Shit." I stared at Lori in shock.

"Indeed. What is worse is studies have shown the DFTD cells are genetically identical to each other."

"Why is that worse?"

"It means the cancer originated from a single individual. And there are entries in our records that suggest it may have been introduced deliberately."

My eyes widened. "For real?"

"Yes."

"By who?"

"We're not sure, but my grandmother believed it was the same group who attempted to eliminate the thylacines."

"The government, you mean?" Miriam crossed her arms.

"There is no evidence of that." Lori closed the file on the tablet.

Miriam lifted a finger. "The government did introduce the bounty on the thylacines."

"Driven by the need to protect the sheep population of the time."

"Says you," Miriam muttered.

The devil Seer slid the tablet back into her bag. "Do I believe there is an intention to eliminate therianthropes? Yes, no doubt. Do I believe it is the work of some overarching government conspiracy? No, I do not. I think the unidentified 'they' have friends and influence in high places."

Miriam rolled her eyes and I nearly laughed out loud. And here I thought adults were responsible and serious and well… grown up.

"Do you think 'they' are responsible for the therianthrope murders?" I asked Miriam.

"If they are, it's not how they normally operate. A bounty on Tigers, a disease in devils, listing the dingo under the Rural Lands Protections Act, where it is subject to government-funded trapping, baiting, and hunting bounties of our own, rather than under the National Parks and Wildlife Act where we belong."

I nearly took a step back at the rising venom in her voice. Quickly, I changed the subject before Miriam got started on her soapbox theme. "Is there a specific reason you're telling me about the devils? Or is it just because I'm a Seer?"

Lori shook her head. "The number of sarcophilus harrisii therianthropes is only ten percent of what it was twenty-five years ago. Like thylacines, we are on the verge of being wiped out. My grandmother wrote that the previous thylacine Seer, Rachel Doherty—"

"Rawdon." My stomach lurched. "Her name was Rachel Rawdon."

"Was it?" Lori frowned. "I thought it was Doherty. Never mind, the point is the previous thylacine Seer was working with my grandmother, attempting to Unlash the thylacine Funem-vitea. When I spoke to Miriam about it the other day, she mentioned you said you read about it."

I could hear the hope in her voice, and I felt about two centimetres tall. This shifter stuff kept getting better and better. The faster I tried to dig my way out, the faster they kept piling stuff on my head. I couldn't even remember when I actually said yes to all this. I sighed. I couldn't exactly back out now.

"Nothing specific, just that there is such a thing. One second." Frowning, I went to my bag and searched through my growing collection of sketchbooks until I found the correct one. The effects on the faces of the devils were freakishly familiar. Nightmarishly, in fact. I opened the book to the page I was thinking of. "You want to Lash the devils, don't you? Keep them human."

"As humans, they don't contract the disease."

"But once infected, the cancer stays, even when they return to human."

I handed the book to Lori. The page was open to the woman with the disfigured face. It wasn't Proteus syndrome like Joseph Merrick; it was DFTD.

Lori looked down at the page and slowly nodded. "Yes. Will you help?"

"On one condition." I held up a finger.

Lori looked up at me and I could see the tears welling in her eyes.

"When we figure out how to Lash the beast, we write it down, and we do not lose it."

Chapter Nineteen

"How can I even think about homework?" I dropped back onto my bed.

Evie and I were in my room with all the English stuff spread out on the bed between us.

"Because it's the normal part of life that keeps you grounded. Besides, don't you want a break from poring over coded history?"

I wanted to get it over and done with and have its ugly, head-rearing mess out of my life, but Evie appeared so comfortable with that entire world it made it impossible to tell her. I made a face at her instead. "It's Shakespeare. It's still coded history."

"Ha, ha. You'll be pleased to know we've now gathered enough information to answer all the questions. All we have left is to pull it together into our presentation."

"Yippee." I rolled my eyes as I sat up again. "How can you read all this stuff anyway? Thees, thous, and wetherforto hibbity-jibbet."

Evie shrugged. "I love the cadence and the sentence structure, and the turn of phrase. Also, helps I'm not dyslexic."

"How is that, by the way? You're a Seer."

"Not a thylacine Seer."

Evie dropped her notepad in her lap and rested her hands on it for a second before she reached up and tucked her hair behind her ears. For the first time, I saw she wore hearing aids.

"You're deaf." For some reason, my hands moved as I spoke. Not usual 'talking with your hands' gestures. I crossed my fingers and tapped my head in the middle of it.

Sitting up straight, Evie stared at me for a second then began to move her hands without speaking. I was stunned to realise I understood her.

"You know sign language?"

I looked down at my hands. "I didn't know I did."

"Let's test this." Evie moved her hands again. *"I'm deaf in the legal sense, but I can still hear sound. I hear at a lower frequency range and a higher frequency range compared to most humans, but without my hearing aids, I'm deaf within the normal range. Because of this, too much sound is overwhelming and incoherent noise. In the Northern Territory, it wasn't too bad, even in Darwin. It's so open there sounds sort of dissipate. We lived in Melbourne for a year and I almost went crazy."*

"Wow. And Miriam's the same?"

"Has hearing issues, yes. She can hear low sounds like you wouldn't believe. High-pitched sounds, not so well."

"We're all odd, from the sounds of it."

"Yes, we are. And I can't believe you know sign language."

"I don't remember ever learning it."

"Could be your instinctual language. Me, I would love to have it as mine, but no, I speak Dutch instead. Helpful the one and only time I helped out some lost tourist back in Palmerston, but not since."

We both jumped a mile when the doorbell rang, and then laughed in unison at our overreaction.

"Are you expecting someone?" Evie asked.

"No." I slid off the bed. "We don't usually get visitors. Two in one day. It's a record."

Heading out to the lounge room, I peered through the peephole then opened the door.

"You were right."

"Well, hello to you too, Josh." Stepping back, I let him in the house, glancing at his bike in the driveway. I hadn't even heard the engine. Dad hadn't said anything about Josh visiting without him home last time, so I figured it was okay. Besides, Evie was here, too. "What was I right about?"

"Rachel's married name was Doherty. The Elders are looking into it now, but you might be the first Seer ever where it's come down through the paternal side of the family."

"Or it could be a complete coincidence."

"No way. That would be…. Tell you what. If you aren't related to Rachel through your dad, I'll give away my season tickets to the Chargers games."

I put my hands on my hips. "There's no need to be drastic. I don't see what the big deal is anyway. It doesn't help us with Lashing the beast, or the murders, or anything useful. Anyway, I didn't expect that you'd go all 'tell it to the Elders' on me. Makes me wonder why I bother telling you stuff in the first place."

"Simple. You want answers."

"I must be asking the wrong questions, because answers about my family line isn't exactly what I'm after."

He lowered his voice a little. "Have you found anything in your dungeon yet?"

I glanced toward my bedroom and shook my head. "Nothing useful on the Lashing. I can't exactly go down there when my dad is at home, you know. Explaining where I've disappeared to could get a little sticky."

"He's not here at the moment, right? They have the training day today. We could totally—"

"Not do anything right now. Evie's here and we're working on school stuff."

"Actually, Evie wants to know about your dungeon." Evie had appeared at the hallway entrance.

"Thanks a lot." I frowned at Josh.

"Don't blame him. Different frequency, remember? I couldn't hear him clearly until he lowered his voice."

For a second, I hesitated. Telling Evie about it all was dumping more Seer-shifter stuff into the pile. But then she was a Seer. It might be a good thing. She could help. With her helping, we could get it all over with faster. I was totally up for that. I opened my mouth then changed my mind and signed instead. It was way cool I could do this sign language thing. *"Josh and I found a secret room with all the Seer Chronicles and stuff."*

"So even though you don't have a Seer to teach you the ropes, you do have a source of knowledge. That's a relief."

"It is?"

"Grandma and I were wondering how we were

going to teach you a lifetime of knowledge when you're a different species."

"Thanks a lot."

"I meant Seer for a different species. Don't get your knickers in a knot. And you know your dad's not home right now, don't you?"

"Yes, so?"

Evie grinned. *"Show me your dungeon."*

Josh snapped his fingers. "Hey, girls, you know I'm standing right here, don't you? If you're going to sign, slow it down so I have at least a chance to understand you."

"You sign?" Evie asked him.

"Basic. I used to watch the signer at church when I was a kid then practiced."

"Awesome."

"What about the homework?" I reminded Evie.

She waved her hand dismissively. "I'll write it up later. We've got next Tuesday to practice the presentation."

"Well look at you, Miss 'homework will keep you grounded'. Are you sure you want to do this?"

"Hell yeah."

Chapter Twenty

"Check it out." Evie gave a low whistle as the lights seeped orange into the shadowed room. "This is amazing. There are so many records. You guys must have a hell of a lot of predictions."

Coming to a standstill as Evie did a slow circle of the room, I frowned at the piles of books on the table. I was sure I'd tidied them up the last time I was here, but one was left open on the table.

"There're not just predictions. There are records of history, family lines, political squabbling with Elders." Josh indicated the various areas as he spoke.

"So, you've been down here a few times then?"

"Once or twice. But most of it I know from listening to Ginny. She's got an amazing memory when it comes to all the details and dates and things. She's doing a brilliant job at starting to piece together this whole thylacine bounty thing, too."

I stared at him as if he were crazy. If any more overblown compliments came rolling off his tongue, I'd have to start mopping them off the floor.

"There's a current bounty on canis lupus, you know?" Evie said.

"Miriam did mention that." I nodded then patted the top of the nearest pile of Chronicles. As much as I was more than ready for this shifter stuff to be out of my life, I'd discovered its start had a crazy cool story. "But was yours started by a jilted lover?"

"Are you serious?"

With a grin at her tone, I patted the pile of Chronicles on the table again. "I don't have all the pieces of the story yet, because it's written in dozens of books all out of order—"

Evie snorted. "Kind of like your sketchbooks. Must be a family trait."

"Are you saying it's in my genes to screw with future generations of Seers?"

"Hmm, maybe."

"Well, obviously I can't mess with tradition." I shrugged.

"Sure thing, Tevye."

"Huh?"

"Never mind. Jilted lover," she prompted.

"I can't confirm a hundred percent, but apparently, Mercy Chisholm, the Seer in 1830, had a fiancé who was starting to get all uppity because she was spending all her time with 'other guys.' Her grandmother had just died, so she was the only Seer at the time, and she didn't have the Elders at that point either. As a committee, they were created later."

"When there wasn't a Seer, right?"

"Nope. Pretty much when the bounty stuff hit the fan. Anyway, her fiancé, who is only referred to as 'EWS,' got all huffy, so she told him. Everything.

The whole therian-whatsit."

"Therianthrope," Josh supplied.

"The whole kit and caboodle. He gets all freaked out and does a runner. Only thing is, he works for the Van Diemen Land's Company, somewhere in management, so I don't think it's a coincidence the same company introduces a bounty on thylacines, in 1830, the very next year."

"And when the government took that bounty to a pound, it got people excited, and Ginny thinks that's when Prudence started to Lash the beast."

"Prudence was seventeen at the time, so she and Mercy were Lashing them."

Evie nodded slowly. "You could be on to something."

"I wished it helped now." I sat at the table. "Sometimes I feel like I'm on a treadmill. Running very fast, but ultimately going nowhere."

Evie sat opposite me and rested her chin on her arms, which she had crossed on the top of the nearest pile of Chronicles. "If it helps, the current theory about the murders is pretty much the same as your jilted lover idea. That someone or a small group of someones has found out about the thylacine therianthropes and is attempting to thin the population."

"Well, I can't help you. There's no record of what happened seven years ago."

I waved my hand, attempting to indicate the Chronicles, and ended up toppling a pile to the floor. Evie helped me collect them and place them on the table, only for me to knock the pile again when I stood up.

"Oh, come off it," I muttered.

"Ginny, wait."

Evie held out her hand to stop me from picking them up again. Squatting beside me, she picked up one book and dropped it to the floor before picking up the next and doing the same thing. She got to book number five before curiosity got the better of me.

"What are you doing?"

She dropped the first book again. "There's something different about this book. It doesn't sound right."

"How do you mean?"

"The others…" She dropped book two and three again, listening. "They have a reverberating echo. This one doesn't."

I looked down at the book she held out in her hand. "They're all different books."

"I know, but this one sounds flat."

"Flat?"

"Just trust me, okay?"

"Okay." I took the book. It was a brown leather book with a well-worn spine. Obviously, this one had been written in or read a lot by previous Seers. I flicked it open to a random page. "This is one of Mercy's. This is the one where she writes about the bounty from the Van Diemen Land's Company."

Opening the Chronicle to the back cover, I checked the inside again. I'd already checked all the Chronicles I had read, but checking it one more time couldn't hurt. The back of the cover was completely flat. No raised ridges to indicate a hidden scrap of paper.

"Do that again."

I frowned. "Do what again?"

"Open the book flat like you just had it."

Slowly, I flattened the book.

191

"What the hell? Can I…?"

I gave her the Chronicle. Evie opened the book wide, touching the two covers together like butterfly wings, sending the pages into a wild fan.

"What are you doing?" I winced. At any second, the book was going to tear apart.

She slid her finger down into the cavity created at the back of the spine, and withdrew a slender wooden tube hanging by a loop of ribbon around her finger. "Finding this."

"What is it?"

"Something hidden, apparently."

The tube was no longer than about three centimetres and maybe about twice as thick as a regular pencil. Evie passed it to me, and I ran my fingers over it. It was smooth and felt nearly warm in my fingers. But then my fingers were at a constant state of cold since moving here that an ice cube probably felt warm these days. Finding a tiny ridge about half a centimetre down, I tugged on the loop of ribbon and a small cap came off, exposing the curled paper inside. It crinkled as I unfurled it.

"*Abaft the knot to cease the Lash.*" I snapped my head up to stare at Josh as he knelt beside me. "Cease the Lash. Do you think—?"

"That this is related to the whole 'Lash the beast' thing? Absolutely."

"But what the hell does it mean?"

"Maybe it means that…" Evie bit her lip. "We really could use your interpreter right now."

"Interpreter?"

"Yeah. Every Seer has one. They're the one person who can understand the meaning in the Seer predictions. You kind of need one to be an effective Seer. I don't suppose you happen to know who yours is. Do you?"

I stared at her for a second with a sinking feeling. Seers needed interpreters? Why the hell did this crap have to get more and more complicated? Just one more thing to try and figure out. Just one more thing to pull me under the avalanche that this world brought with it. Just one more thing to add to the ever-growing list of Seer duties that must be done. Just one more puzzle piece I couldn't solve. Josh was better at....

The sinking feeling bounced back so fast with startled realisation I was honestly surprised I didn't hit the roof.

Slowly, I nodded. "Yeah, I think I might."

"Who?" Josh frowned at me.

"Duh. You."

"Me?"

"You figured out the train derailment. You understood how to write the code. You know the girl I drew. Who else would it be?"

"I don't think...." Josh looked like I'd hit him in the head with a two-by-four. "Shit, you could be right."

"Of course I'm right." I handed him the slip of paper. "Now if you'd be so kind as to figure this out, that would be great."

He held the paper with two hands. "If I'm your interpreter, why can't I read the Seer code?"

Evie held up her hands. "Don't look at me. This code is a thylacine thing. We don't use it."

"What did this say again?" He moved closer and pointed down at the page.

Leaning on the chair, I peered at it in his hand. *"Abaft the knot to cease the Lash."*

"Abaft? What does that mean?"

I shrugged. "Don't look at me."

"I don't know either, but it does sound like an old English word."

Josh pulled out his phone. "How is it spelled?"

Again, I shrugged. "It's code. It doesn't give me the spelling."

"Not really helping me here," Josh grumbled.

"Sorry."

I bit my lip, wondering if he was upset or not. When he moved closer to the entryway so he had reception and began typing on his phone without further mutterings, I figured he wasn't. I turned back to Evie. "Who is your interpreter?"

"Michael Shephard. He's back in Palmerston. It was the only way the therianthropes would let both Grandma and me come here. We Skype them every other day with predictions, and they tell us what is going on."

"Are all interpreters guys?"

With a shrug, Evie stood up and started placing the Chronicles back on the table. "So, with this many books, I must ask, and I know you do write yours down like we do. But, how often do you have predictions?"

It was my turn to shrug. "Sometimes, it'll be five or six in a day for a few days, but then there'll be nothing for weeks. You?"

"About the same. I think it's cool you draw yours. I hear mine. It's a hissing whisper that will not go away until I say the words out loud, and then I have to write them down fast before I forget."

I sat back in the chair. "That's interesting."

"What is?"

"Reading has to do with my eyes, and I struggle with that, but I see my predictions like images that block my vision and won't go away until I draw it."

"I struggle to hear, and mine are audible. I wonder what it is for the Sarcophilus harrisii?"

"To the rear of."

I jerked around at Josh's unexpected announcement.

Evie didn't miss a beat. "I hardly think that's a practical area for predictions."

"Abaft. A nautical term that means 'to the rear of,' 'to the aft' or 'behind.'" He put his phone back in his pocket and returned to the table.

"To the rear of the knot to cease the Lash?" I frowned. "Like that makes any sense."

"To the rear…?" Josh whispered.

"Maybe… maybe there's a particular knot you have to untie to unleash…" Evie snapped her fingers. "The Funem-vitea. What's the bet the Funem-vitea has a knot in it? That's the Lashing. It's not a whip; it's a knot."

"To the rear…?" Josh whispered again. "To the rear…?"

"You're starting to sound like a broken record," I teased him.

He ignored me and walked to the other side of the room, looking at the tapestry.

"It's a nautical term. To the rear of the knot."

"It has sailing ships." Hurriedly, I got up and stood at his side.

"And a knot."

Evie came to join us as Josh reached out and moved the edge of the tapestry to the side. He struggled, and we both went to help him. The material was heavier than it looked. And filthy.

Evie sneezed. "Eww, ick. Ginny, you really do need to sack your maid."

"Why? Are you looking for a job?"

Her only answer was a scowl.

The earth wall behind the tapestry was expected. The safe-looking compartment was not. The small, steel rectangular door had no handle, just a dial located centrally within the steel, with twelve small holes around the edge.

"Looks like an old-fashioned telephone." Evie spoke between sneezes. "Who are you going to call?"

Josh made sure we had hold of the tapestry then let go to run his hand along the edge of the safe. "Well certainly not *Ghostbusters*. There're images here. Look."

I shoved my part of the tapestry further along so I could turn and lean the weight of it against my back. I didn't know fabric could be so heavy. Josh reached into his pocket and pulled out his phone, turning on his torch function and shining it on the dial.

"A seahorse, a monkey, a fish, a cow…." He looked at me and tapped his phone lightly on my arm. "Do these animals seem familiar to you?"

"Is there a grasshopper and a kangaroo?"

Josh aimed his torch back at the door. "Yes."

"The clock," both he and I spoke together.

"What clock?" Evie asked.

"A drawing I did."

Josh turned back to me. "Do you have the sketchbook?"

"Upstairs, but you might not need it. I distinctly remember that the animals were drawn in alphabetical order—"

"Starting at the one o'clock position. You're right."

"So, what? We move the animals somehow?" Evie's tone was sceptical. "Where's Noah Wyle when you need him?"

"Who?"

Evie shook her head at me. "Never mind."

"I don't think the animals move, but..." Josh placed his finger at the dial where one o'clock would be on a clock and moved it around until he aligned with the image of the bee.

"Something clicked into place." Evie jerked up straight then quickly moved back down before she lost her grip on the tapestry.

When Josh moved his hand away from the dial, it stayed on the bee for a second before it spun back to the start with a dull ratchet sound.

"What's next?"

"There's an elephant." Evie nodded.

"Cow," I corrected. "A, B, C, D, E. Cow comes first."

"Oh good." Evie grinned at me. "I'm not the only one who has to sing the alphabet song to get it in the right order."

Josh dialled two o'clock around to the cow then looked at Evie.

"Yep." She nodded.

"You are going to tell me about this super hearing you've got, one day, right?" He released the dial then moved onto the three o'clock and the elephant.

"I wouldn't say it's super. Irritating and disturbing, sure. I think the fish would be the next animal."

Josh dialled.

"F. G. Grasshopper would be after that," I told him.

"H. Horse," Evie added.

Josh continued to dial, while Evie and I attempted to get the order correct.

"I. Nothing. J. Nothing."

"K...." Evie trailed off as we both looked.

"Kangaroo. L?"

"Lizard. M."

"Monkey. N. Nothing O. Octopus. P. Noth—"

"Platypus. Q."

"No. R. And, seahorse would be the last one. Right?" I did a check of the animals again.

"I think so," Evie said as Josh dialled the twelve around to the seahorse and released it to ratchet back to its original place. "Something is whirring in there."

The centre of the dial opened in a spin to reveal a black metal button etched with a sailing ship.

"I'd say we got it right." Josh glanced at me. "Ginny, do you want to do the honours?"

"Love to. But I can't while I'm hanging onto this tapestry."

"I could swap places with you."

"Push the button, Josh."

"Are you sure? It's your safe."

I glared at him. Holding this thing wasn't easy, but Evie spared me the comment.

"Do what she says, Josh. This tapestry is heavy."

Josh pushed the button. The door swung open and revealed a cavity with a carved wooden box. Reaching inside, he carefully pulled it out, closing the safe so Evie and I could drop the tapestry.

"I think they used lead and gold thread in that." Evie sneezed twice more. "A ton of it."

I couldn't believe how light I suddenly felt. It

was surprising I didn't float. Instead, I overbalanced and landed heavily on the wall to the right of the tapestry. Something dug into my shoulder.

"Ouch."

"What the…?"

My head snapped towards Evie at her cry, but she was staring at the tapestry. Instinctively, I jumped away and landed somewhere near her side. Even I could hear the ratchet sounds now as it started to move, and we watched it ease its way to the left, leaving the wall bare.

Slowly, I took a few steps forward and ran my hand over the smooth, rounded, black half sphere jutting from the wall encasing the small white switch poking out like a forgotten Tic Tac.

"That would have been useful before."

"Another door."

Evie's voice was a whisper as Josh crossed to the wooden door to the left of the safe the tapestry had revealed and eased the handle down. It stuck for a few seconds before he managed to coax it open. We gathered around to peer down the earth carved corridor disappearing into the darkness.

"What is this place?" Josh asked. "Wonderland?"

"Narnia. We are in the back of Ginny's wardrobe."

Josh tilted his head in a way that made me think he thought Evie's comment was fair enough. "So, box or door?"

"Ginny?"

I wished she hadn't put it on me. I eyed the dark corridor, feeling as though yet another thing in this mad mess had literally been opened in front of me. I was starting to feel like there would never be an end to it. Glancing at the box in Josh's hand, I suppressed a sigh.

"Box, I suppose. After all, we did just work out a puzzle safe. I think we've earned it."

Chapter Twenty-One

Josh placed the box on the table and propelled me by the shoulders to the chair.

"Sit. This one you get to do."

I stumbled down onto the chair, caught by surprise. "Oh okay, sure."

Evie took the seat opposite, and Josh crouched down to my right with his arms crossed on the table. I pulled the box closer, caught in the web of expectation. The carving of the outside of the box was all swirly patterns. After the detail on the safe, I expected it to have animals and ships on it too. I ran my hands over the box and found two small wooden hinges on one side. After inspecting the lid on the opposite side, I found the little lip I could catch my finger under. The lid opened normally. I was half expecting a trick of some sort, but I did need Josh's help to open it completely. It was, after all, a wooden box that hadn't been opened in years. Inside, four stiff leather triangles attached to each of the four sides overlapped at the top of the box, I assumed to protect the contents. I flipped them out over the sides of the box. Inside was more leather, softer and not quite so dark. As I pulled it out, Josh moved the box aside to give me room. It was a leather envelope tied together with leather straps so thin I was worried I was going to break them when I undid the knots. Obviously, leather was sturdier material than I thought.

Okay, now my heart was pounding like I was going to find diamonds or something. From the look on their faces, it was probable they thought the same. I gave a quick grin to ease the building tension, but the others didn't notice. Their eyes were laser focused on the package. Once it was untied and opened out, we all looked down at the exposed sheets of paper. They weren't like any paper I had ever seen. It was thick and soft, moulding over my fingers when I picked the first page up.

"Oh my gosh." Evie reached out and ran her hand over the parchment. "I've never heard paper sound like that."

"You hear paper?" Josh shifted so he could kneel rather than stay crouched.

"I'm sure you do, too." Evie closed her eyes and moved her hands as though hearing what she spoke. "The slide of your hand over a page. The rub of two together when you separate them to turn a page. The crinkle when you fold an edge, or the flick when you attempt to straighten one out."

"You make reading a book sound so seductive." Josh shook his head.

"Sorry." Evie's eyes flew open. "What I'm saying is different paper has different sounds. This doesn't sound like paper. It sounds more like leather."

I turned the first page over. It had nothing on it,

front or back. The second page was another story altogether.

"Wow." I gave a low whistle. The shading on the images was amazing. Even though it was black faded ink on a pale tan leather, everything was finely detailed and nearly three-dimensional. It was almost as if the individual drawings were about to walk off the page.

"Far out. That's a little…" Evie cleared her throat. "…well endowed."

It was only then I took in what the image was. An exceedingly anatomically correct drawing of a naked man dominated the centre of the page. He was shown as if walking from left to right, with his left leg stepping forward and his right leg stepping back, pretty much showing everything. Seven animals were drawn around his body attached to various areas by what appeared to be glowing strands.

"That's a numbat." Evie pointed to the little long-nosed creature with stripes like a thylacine and a long tapering tail. The animal was attached by the glowing strand to the head of the man. "And a wombat."

The fat, furry wombat was attached to the strand connecting to his chest.

"Thylacine and dingo." Josh pointed to the animals attached to the torso and stomach respectively.

"Is that a kangaroo attached to his foot?" Evie peered at the page. "Or a wallaby?"

"A kangaroo, I think." I pointed to the animal attached to the small of his back. "A devil."

"And a bat." Josh named the final animal seeming attached to the man's back between his shoulders. "I think that's the odd one out. The rest are all native to Australia."

"It could be a flying fox," Evie pointed out. "They're native."

"Torso, stomach, and the small of his back are the three therian... shifters. Is it possible all seven of them are?"

Evie ran her finger along the strand connecting the numbat to his head. "That would make the strands Funem-vitea. I suppose it's possible."

"I've never heard of other therianthropes."

"That's not saying much." Evie rested her chin in her hand and looked across at Josh. "Your Elders didn't know what a Funem-vitea was, and that's kind of important."

I moved on to the next page before an argument could start. The naked man was back, and this time there was a naked woman with him. The man was facing away, revealing his back, and the woman had the strand connected to the flying fox resting in her hand.

"She's the Seer," I gasped.

"How can you tell?" Evie leaned closer.

I hovered my hand over the woman's face, pointing out what was obvious. "Her eyes are purple. It's the only touch of colour on the page."

"It's not just colour." Josh carefully lifted the edge of the page. "Check it out. It looks like extremely thin slivers of some sort of stone."

"That's unbelievable." Evie took the page to look closer. "How the heck do you think they did that?"

"Carefully," I muttered, but I wasn't paying too much attention to my answer. The next page immediately pulled my focus.

There were three different sets of drawings on this page. In the first one, the entire flying fox was inlaid with a pale stone, but with enough detail drawn ever so carefully around it that the animal was still clearly recognisable. The Seer, again with the purple stone in her eyes, had her hand against the back of the naked man.

The second image was nearly identical, except the human and flying fox were in reverse. The man was now inlaid with pale stone with added ink detail, and the flying fox was a completely drawn image. The woman was drawn the same as in the first image but was now turned while her hand was close to touching the flying fox.

The third image was different. It had the man and the flying fox, but as distant images in the background bringing the main image to the front and centre of the drawing. A slender hand, which looked feminine to me, was holding a thread with her thumb and forefinger as if she was running her hand along it.

"How much are you willing to bet the pale stone represents the Silver?" I asked.

"If I didn't know any better, I'd say that was depicting a forced walk."

"I think you're right, Evie." Carefully, I picked up the page and turned it over to join the growing pile to my left, checking first it didn't have anything on the back. It didn't.

The next page was similar to the last one. It had three images centrally on the page. The first and second images were identical to the previous page. The third was different. Instead of a hand simply running along the strand, it showed a twisted knot in her palm. And there were more images. Nine smaller squares running along the bottom of the page were step-by-step images showing the knot being created.

"Well, what do you know, Evie? You were right." Josh looked up at her. "It is a knot."

"How do we know this is the Lashing though?" I lifted the page.

"What else could it be?" Evie's green eyes were wide when she looked up at me.

I didn't answer. Knowing my luck, it would be the start of a new trail to follow, deepening the spiral downwards. I checked there was nothing on the back of that page as I turned it over on the pile.

The final page under it showed two images. Both had the flying fox, the man, and the Seer back into play. The first image showed the flying fox as the Silver. The Seer held her hand with the knot near the man. The second image also showed the flying fox as the Silver. The Seer held her hand with the knot near the flying fox and a single stroke had been slashed across the image in ink.

Josh stood up and leaned on the table, casting a shadow over the pages of leather. Even under his shadow, the thin pieces of pale stone in the Silver shimmered a ghostly light. I shut my eyes for a second. Okay, now I was getting carried away.

He tapped the image without the slash running through it. "So, that would mean the Lashing only works against what is in transition at the time. If you want to lash the beast in human form, you have to tie the knot while we're in human form."

"Again…" I placed the page showing the how-to of the knot in front of us. "How do we know this is the Lashing?"

"There's only one way to find out." Josh

grinned as he took the final page and stared down at it.

"Yeah, but Ginny needs to un-Lash you first. How does she do that?"

Very gently, Josh put the page he held down and carefully flipped the leather that had bound the pages in the first place. "Probably, like this."

The back of the leather had three more images on it.

"How'd you know that was there?" I stared down at it.

"I saw it when you pulled it out of the box."

Again, the flying fox was the Silver, and the male was drawn in ink. The Seer held her hands on both sides of the knot which was now centralised along the strand. The next drawing showed a close up of the knot between her hands, and the final showed her hands further apart and the Funem-vitea a single, unknotted strand.

"Do you think she pulls it?" Evie asked.

"Hello." Josh waved his hand. "Willing test dummy right here."

"If this isn't what we think it is, it could be…."

I couldn't think of the words. I could only stare down at the pile of leather, trying to ease the flash of fear burning through me.

"Disastrous to your health," Evie supplied.

"What she said," I whispered.

"I'm willing to take that risk."

He might be, but I sure as heck wasn't. "Why like this?"

"What do you mean?" Evie asked.

"This." I pointed to the leathers, the box, and then to the safe. "Why the hints and clues and treasure hunt? Why the secrecy? They started

Lashing thylacine in 1888. They could have had no idea the Seer line would continue, or that all their records would stay here. What if Rachel had moved? Why not write it down so the next Seer would know what to do? They hid it, and Prudence didn't show Rachel."

I ran my hands frustratedly through my hair, pulling a few strands from my plait as it did so. Josh and Evie merely blinked at me.

"Didn't you tell me Rachel was born in 1908?" Josh asked quietly.

"Yeah, so?"

"Prudence was murdered in 1910. Rachel would have been two. She couldn't have shown her anything."

"Not my point."

Evie rested her elbows on the table and placed her chin in her hands. "So, what is your point?"

"My point is…" I took a calming breath, aware my words came out in a near growl. "They hid the instructions. They didn't leave them in plain sight. They didn't make them easy to find."

"So?"

I glared at Josh. "So? Don't you think there could be a good reason for it? That it could be dangerous?"

They were both silent for a second, and I could see my words sinking in. Finally.

"Maybe we should wait until we can attempt it with the Elders." Evie's words were quiet in the silence.

"What are they going to do?" Josh stood. "They can't access the Funem-vitea."

"She does have a point though, Josh. If something does go wrong, it's not like we can get emergency services down here."

"If something goes wrong, do you think you'd *want* emergency services down here?"

"Not the point." I gathered the pages together in the right order and started to pack them away. I needed something to do.

"Alright, so we go back to Ginny's room. Come on. You want a practice run, right? Before you do the big reveal in front of the others?"

I froze, unable to process his words for a long moment. "Are you bloody stupid? Are you really that keen to risk your life?"

"I'm that keen to be free." He pushed his hair back off his face. "You don't understand, do you? A part of me is being denied. Can you imagine if you were told you could never draw again unless it was with an orange pen, and then all manufacturers stopped making them? On the very rare occasions you did find an orange pen, someone would come along and stop you before you finished drawing and hide your pen."

"Why would they hide it, Josh? Tell me, if it isn't dangerous, why would they go to all that trouble?" I glared at him, and he glared at me. Neither of us willing to back down.

"So it wouldn't fall into the wrong hands." Both Josh and I turned slowly to Evie, as she sat up and tapped the pile of Chronicles. "Well, think about it. Codes are all well and good, but codes are breakable. You did say Prudence was murdered, right?"

She waited until both Josh and I nodded before she continued.

"Maybe, somehow if this knowledge got into the wrong hands at the time, it could have made things worse. There could have been a bigger threat back then. But that was over a hundred years ago. Whoever those wrong hands were, they're not around now. Even Lashed, thylacines continued, right? Cornelia, Monty, Barbara, Josh, all born therianthropes, even though it's been two or three generations of Lashed thylacines. Lashing them didn't kill them. I'm sure Unlashing them won't either."

Two against one. And there was no way I could win this. No way I could convince them. It wasn't my fault if this all came down on our heads like a ton of bricks.

"Don't blame me if this—"

"We won't." Josh's eyes never left my face, and I could see his smile the second I admitted defeat.

"Okay. My room. Let's go."

Chapter Twenty-Two

My room wasn't big, and with all three of us standing between the wardrobe and the bed, it felt tiny. Evie bounced onto the bed, narrowly missing all the papers and books.

"Let's do this," she nearly squealed. "It's starting to get exciting."

"Exciting isn't the word I'd use."

Ignoring my muttering, Josh grabbed my hands and practically dragged me to the other side of the room, near my desks. "There's more room here."

"Are you sure you want to do this?" I tried again, one last time.

"Absolutely."

"No responsibility or liability shall be accepted on the part of the Seer in the event of any damage or loss, partial or in its entirety."

"Yeah, yeah, we get that." Evie laughed.

I wasn't joking. I was terrified something horrible was about to happen.

Josh pushed his hair back off his face and lowered his hands to his side. It was obvious he was ready. I looked at him then down at his Silver. His Silver was staring at me, literally quivering on all fours. I was pretty sure my Silver was quivering, too, but not for the same reasons. It was almost impossible to close the distance between Josh and me. My legs didn't want to move. Josh did it for me instead. Stepping forward, he placed my hand at his solar plexus.

"You can do this. I trust you."

This had nothing to do with trust.

"Do you want the instructions?" Evie waved the leather page at me. The one with the knot-tying directions.

"Unlashing, not Lashing. Yet," Josh told her. I was staring at my hand on his torso and moved my head to follow the gentle finger he placed at my chin until I was looking up at him. "It's going to be okay."

Swallowing hard, I nodded and tried to ignore the image of him collapsing and frantic phone calls for the ambulance. Hidden for safekeeping, like Evie said. That was all. Looking back down, I pulled my hand away. It tingled and glowed. I had the knot. I took a stumbled step backwards, and it took me a few more seconds until I could take the shaking steps across the room, placing myself between Josh and his Silver. Carefully, I lowered my hand, hoping to detangle myself from the Funem-vitea I couldn't see. My hand came away from the glow and it kind of hung there in midspace. It was freakishly alien hovering in the air like that.

I glanced at Josh. "Do you feel okay?"

"Yup."

My gaze returned to the glow and I took a deep breath. "Here goes nothing."

I held my hands to either side of it where I guessed the Funem-vitea to be. I couldn't feel anything like string to indicate where it was, but there was a slight tingle, less than when I held the glow, but enough to notice. Inching my hands slowly, I moved them so the tingle was inside my closed fists, squeezed tightly, and eased both hands apart. The glow became smaller. It was working. I kept pulling until the glow disappeared altogether.

Josh gasped and fell to his knees.

"Josh." I knelt at his side, a surge of frantic fear setting my heartbeat into a drumbeat in my head.

"I'm okay." His voice sounded strangled. "Just give me a sec."

"Oh shit."

No other words came as a pulsing light shot across the room from Josh to his Silver. With each pulse, the thylacine became more solid, until it no longer appeared as a translucent ghost, but an animal of liquid silver. I almost expected it to leave a puddle when it moved. It didn't. Instead, the liquid silver seeped across the room, wrapping itself into a strand shape until it hit Josh in the chest. It sent him flying from a kneeling position and he crashed into my mirror stand, smacking it into the wall, and sending jewellery and glass everywhere.

"Josh!"

I was frozen. I couldn't move. He lay still. He wasn't—

"Ouch." He slowly sat up with a wince and I collapsed with a thud onto the carpet.

"That was cool," Evie spoke deadpan from the bed. "But still seven years' bad luck."

"If this worked, it's a fair deal," he told her.

"Careful." It was the only word that came

through the mix of relief and retreating adrenaline. He hesitated and looked at me for a second. Clearing, my throat, I tried again. "There's glass everywhere."

"Still better than if I'd hit the desk." He started to get up.

"If you say so. There's going to be glass in my carpet for weeks."

"Months." Evie shrugged when I glanced at her. "Just saying."

"Are you sure you're okay?" Only now was I able to find some strength in my rubbery legs to attempt standing again.

"Yeah. A few bruises maybe, but I'm all good."

Evie sat upright. "So… the million-dollar question. Did it work?"

"Let me clean up before we try it out, please. Josh has shoes, but his thylacine doesn't. Not really keen on attempting to explain how I got a supposedly extinct animal's blood in my room."

"Ginny, get duct-tape and the vacuum cleaner. Josh and I will pick up the big pieces."

"Duct-tape?"

"Trust me."

I'd never seen someone clean glass so fast. The duct-tape to the carpet trick worked far too well, and I had no excuses left. It wasn't the shifting I dreaded. I'd seen him do it twice before, and I'd seen the Elders and the others do it. It was shifting after I'd muddled with the balance of things. There was no way of telling what would happen now. The drawings could mean something entirely different. Maybe Josh was going to turn into a flying fox. Maybe once he shifted, he would never be able to change back.

A flash of light ran from the thylacine to Josh and it was too late. The thylacine was standing in the room where Josh had been, and a liquid silver Josh took its place. Quickly, I averted my eyes, but then noticed there was no pile of clothes next to the thylacine. Slowly, I looked up again. For the first time, Josh's Silver wore clothes. The same clothes he'd been wearing, just washed over in a Silver liquid shimmer.

"It worked." Evie pumped the air. "Yes."

The thylacine stretched with its back arched and its front legs out straight and gave a huge yawn before inspecting my room.

Evie pulled a face. "Yikes. Teeth. That's kind of scary."

"Tell me about it." I watched the thylacine as I spoke. "If you start pawing through my dirty laundry or marking territory, there'll be hell to pay."

The thylacine turned its head toward me and gave me a pointed look. I grinned. There was no doubt he understood.

I blinked in slow realisation at what I was seeing. "Bloody hell."

"What?"

"He's crystal clear."

"And that means…?"

"He's not blurry. Thylacine are blurry when they Beast Walk."

"Seriously?"

"Yeah. Didn't you notice it with the Elders?"

"Now, that you mention it… they were blurry. He's definitely not."

Josh's human Silver leaned against my desk, and I went over to inspect it. Slowly, I moved my hand through it. It felt exactly the same. Warm air and nothing else. To tell the truth, I was relieved. I was half expecting the whole *Matrix* 'cover the hand and seep up the arm' deal. I released a slow breath I hadn't been aware of holding. So far, so good.

"Now for the real test."

I turned my head to Evie. "Huh?"

"Can he change back?"

A flash moved between the beast and the Silver, and Josh spoke from where the thylacine had entered my wardrobe. He poked his head out. "The real question is does he want to? Ginny, could you—"

"You're wearing them, Josh." I told him calmly from the desk with a small smile.

He looked down at himself for the first time. "I'm wearing clothes?"

"Yup." I couldn't help grinning at the stunned-mullet expression on his face. In fact, I had the nearly uncontrollable urge to laugh.

Josh stood and stepped out of the wardrobe still looking down at himself. "I'm wearing clothes. Hell, yeah, I can get used to this."

Evie gave an excited squeal and started doing a wiggle dance on the bed. "This is so awesome. Ginny Unlashed the Beast. Ginny Unlashed the Beast."

I was more relieved than excited, like I'd passed a test but was too exhausted from studying for it to penetrate.

"Did you find anything interesting in your look around?" I circled my finger.

Frowning, Josh shook his head. "I was testing my senses. Everything is sharper, louder, stronger. You seem to put your perfume on when you're standing in front of where your mirror was. It's strongest over there, and there's still some glass under your desk. Are you sure you don't own a dog?"

"Yeah, why?"

He screwed up his face. "There is a really strong scent of dog."

"Maybe Rachel did?"

"It's too strong to be that long ago, but maybe." He shrugged.

Evie cleared her throat and waved her hand at us. "Maybe it's Ginny."

"What?" Evie's words hit my head like a drop of blood into water, writhing messily where only clarity should have been. I crossed my arms. "Are you saying I stink like dog?"

"No, but I am saying you are a canis lupus."

Another drop of blood and my skin prickled with unease. It was exactly what I didn't want her to say. Josh's shake of his head allowed me to release the grip on my crossed arms.

"There's definitely her scent here, too. It's not the same."

"Okay. And everyone in your family smells the same in human as they do in Beast?"

"No," he said slowly. "They have two separate scents."

"That's what I thought. So, maybe it is Ginny."

I tried to take a step back, only to smack into the desk. It jolted my weight and made me stumble. I had to uncross my arms to grab the edge like I intended to hoist my hip up onto it the whole time. "That's impossible. I've never... I don't... I've only ever been human."

"One way to find out."

I stared at Evie and crossed my arms again. I

couldn't get any further away from her, and the door was on the other side of the room. "There is no way I'm letting you... no, don't even think about it."

"Okay." She shrugged. "No worries. Just thought you might want to find out if you've been transitioning in your sleep or anything. It's not uncommon for kids to do that, and since you've not been mentored...."

"That is not going to work."

Shift in my sleep? Okay, now I'd heard enough. I couldn't swim fast enough against the tide of the shifter world invading my life. This wasn't what I wanted. At all. Maybe if I closed my eyes long enough, I could wake up in a world where everything made sense. Maybe Josh had it wrong. Maybe Evie was wrong. Maybe there was another explanation.

"Okay, fine." Evie shrugged again. "So, what do we do now? Tell your Elders and get everyone to stand in line for Ginny to Unlash them?"

Josh sat in my desk chair. "It might not be that simple."

Evie crossed her legs. "Why not?"

"Thylacines are considered extinct. Can you imagine what would happen if dozens of us appeared once we can Beast Walk?"

"Zoos and breeding programs, probably."

"And that's the good stuff."

"You think I shift in my sleep?" Both of them stopped talking and looked at me. It was only then I realised they'd been having a different conversation.

I watched Evie place her elbows on her knees and her chin on her hands. "It's a possibility. Yes."

"Why?"

"Instinct."

"Therianthropes have two distinct sides," Josh explained. "A human and a Beast. A left and a right. You might be left-handed, but you have to use your right sometimes. It's how it works."

"So, is that why, even when Lashed, you could still shift when threatened?"

"That's the theory, yes."

I pointed at Evie, an idea forming in my mind. If neither Josh nor Evie were wrong, then this might stop the shifter world from advancing long enough for me to extract myself free. "And you can Lash me so I don't... unless threatened."

"Apparently, now I can."

"Why don't you want to Beast Walk, Ginny?"

I had so many explanations for that right now, and only snippets of thoughts came close enough to voice. It took a few seconds before I lifted my head slowly to look Josh in the eyes. "Because I'm human and I'd like to stay that way. It's bad enough I'm a Seer. I don't need the rest of the crap as well."

"Bad enough? Crap? Is that what you honestly think?" Josh's soft words were almost too casual.

"Come on, Josh. You have to admit all this isn't...."

"Isn't... what?" He spoke in the same tone.

"I don't know. Normal. Natural. Whatever. It's all... supernatural weird stuff."

The casual changed into a band of steel. "Don't hold back. Tell us what you really think. Freaks? Demons? Things possessed? That's us, right? Therianthropes, the abominations that walk this earth."

"Whoa, Josh." Evie patted the air between us. "Calm down, okay? We're all friends here. If you don't know this all exists, of course it'll be all

219

spooky and unsettling. Ginny's only new to this. Give her a break."

He stood up and stalked to my window with crossed arms. When he spoke, it was still in that same soft tone. "Whatever you think we are, Ginny, just remember one thing. You are one of us, too."

My anger surged and it was a struggle to keep my voice calm. I managed it. Barely. "Just because I don't want to shift, Josh, doesn't mean I think you're a freak, or whatever. You love the Beast Walk. I get that. But it doesn't mean I have to."

"It doesn't mean you have to throw it all away either." He turned back to face us. "You don't even know what you're giving up."

I nearly couldn't complete the deep, slow breath keeping my temper on its leash. "Isn't it better that I don't know?"

"Better? No. Easier? Sure. The coward's way out. Absolutely."

"I'm not a coward." Between gritted teeth, the words came out on a hiss.

"But you are possibly the only Seer... the only Seer in history... to be a therianthrope. Unique. Unexplored."

"And I don't get a choice?" Surging to my feet, I stormed over and poked a hard finger at his chest. "I'm not you, Josh. I didn't grow up in a family where you all understood and supported each other. I grew up in a place where my uniqueness got me sent to a shrink, where my uniqueness got me suspended from school, not once, but twice, where the one thing I had any passion for wasn't good enough. 'Stop drawing, Ginny. Study harder, Ginny. You can read, just try harder. You'll be useless if you don't go to university.' Well uniqueness can go jump, for all I frigging care. Just once, just once, I'd like to be normal. Is that too much to ask? Is it?"

Josh didn't back off. In fact, he took a step closer. "So, you're ready to throw it all away on some bizarre notion that 'normal' is the be all and end all of what life is allowed to offer? Sorry to break it to you, Ginny, but you're not normal. Never have been and never will be. Square peg, round hole, and you'll never fit. Please don't waste your life trying. You'll only end up angry at the world and empty inside."

I wasn't ready to back down either. "And you think that a Beast Walk is the answer? That it'll convince me normal isn't what I want? What the hell gives you the right? This is my life."

"This doesn't just affect you, Ginny. It's me and my family, every thylacine therianthrope out there. It affects Evie and Miriam and the canis lupus therianthropes. What you do matters. Like it or not, you are important to more than just yourself. You limit yourself to an orange pen, and you limit everyone. So, yeah, it sucks, but maybe you don't get a choice. You're a Seer and a therianthrope. Denying who you are won't change that."

I stared at him, his angry words swirling around the room like a whirlpool, slamming into everything I wanted to keep. Nothing was safe from the raw abrasion of his words. The whirlpool pulled the plug on my anger, draining it until not a single drop remained, leaving me feeling empty and like something important had slipped away.

"That's not fair, Josh." With that whisper, there was nothing I could do against the fall of tears. I couldn't stop them this time.

"I know it's not." His warm breath puffed

against my neck as his arms came around me.

He was so warm, but I was ice inside. I'd shattered, and he was the only thing keeping the pieces from falling. A dull rushing filled my head, and I felt slightly off balance for a second. One phrase repeated over and over in my mind. I whispered it against his shoulder.

"If anyone finds out I'm not normal, they'll lock me away for good."

"Far out." Evie's hushed tone was full of shock, and I unwillingly pulled away from Josh to see what it was. "That's not something you see every day."

"What's not?" Josh frowned.

"Whenever a canis lupus therianthrope is about to transition into a Beast Walk, a pulsing light runs from the human to the Silver. It happened then for Ginny, except it stopped and faded bare millimetres away from her. Like it ran into a brick wall or something. Can it be you're already Lashed?"

Her words sent a bolt of electricity right through me.

"Only a Seer can do that, right?" Josh's arms slowly fell away from me, almost as if he was reluctant to let me go, and I shivered at the loss of his warmth.

"That's what I assume from those drawings." Evie stood from the bed. "I certainly didn't know what Lashing was before a few weeks ago, and I'm positive Grandma didn't either. Neither of us have met you before, at least I don't think so."

"So, who could have done it?

Josh's question went unanswered as Evie crept across the room and crouched down with her hand held out. I could only assume she was reaching for my Silver. With a look of pure concentration, she followed her outstretched hand until she nearly touched my stomach.

"It's one continuous line. There's no knot I can see."

"If anyone finds out…." Josh whispered. "Is it possible Ginny is blocking it herself?"

"What?" Evie stood up and put her hands on her hips.

"Hear me out." Josh pointed his forefingers to the ceiling, apparently trying to figure it out. "You said, 'If anyone finds out, they'll lock me away.' What if, as a kid, you so desperately wanted to be normal, and were so terrified someone would find out, you have blocked yourself from transitioning?"

The dull rushing came again, and I quickly held the edge of the desk to keep myself from falling. "If I ever transitioned as a kid, I'd remember it."

"Not necessarily."

"Josh is right. It's like people who've been abused or were in horrific car accidents. As a defence mechanism, their brain blocks it out."

"If that's the case, wouldn't I have stopped myself from drawing the future?"

Evie shrugged. "Obviously not."

"And it would explain why you might possibly transition in your sleep. That defence mechanism in your mind shuts down then. You have to realise it's okay to Beast Walk. We're not going to think you're crazy."

"And we certainly are not going to lock you up."

"You can stop now. Both of you. I did my time with a professional shrink. I don't need two amateurs psychoanalysing me." I was only holding it together with a hope and a prayer. If they kept pushing, I was going to crack.

"Well, maybe you are crazy then, but it's a good thing. We wouldn't fit in with normal people. I see things that aren't there, I hear things that no one else does, I don't hear things I'm supposed to, and half the time, I go into a trance-like state and sprout gobbledygook. At least you've got a near photographic memory and an amazing drawing talent thrown in with your crazy."

Josh nodded. "And I transition occasionally into a declared extinct carnivorous marsupial. If I'm ever seen in Beast Walk, half the world would go crazy and put me in a cage. You, however, might get an 'ohh' and an 'ahh,' a few photographs from a distance if you're unlucky, but mostly you'll be left alone."

"So, it's not all bad, right?" Evie grinned at me.

I opened my mouth to remind them it wasn't all good either, when the rushing came again. This time, I couldn't keep my balance and fell.

Flashes of black-and-white images seared across my mind and muffled voices assaulted my ears. Everything was a tangle, and my senses took in more than I could stand. Sudden, searing, cramping pain in my left hand made me jerk up. I was sitting on my bed against the pillows with a sketchpad in my lap and a pencil in my hand.

This didn't make any sense.

Blinking, I looked up and saw Dad in the doorway. Evie was on the end of the bed, and Josh was sitting on the desk chair.

"…and Ginny said the only way I could stay was to help with their homework." Josh shrugged. "So, I'm helping."

"So, how's the assignment going, Ginny?"

I stared numbly at Dad for a second. "I'm confused."

Evie laughed. "Shakespeare. It'll do it to the best of us."

Dad made a face. "I'll leave you to it. Are you two staying for dinner? It'll be tacos."

"I'll have to go shortly." Josh checked his watch.

"Tacos sound good. I'll have to let my mum know."

"Tacos for three coming right up."

Dad disappeared. The others were like statues for a second after he left until Evie dropped the book she was holding and scrambled up the bed next to me.

"Ginny, are you okay?"

"My hand is killing me, but otherwise I'm okay. What happened?"

"You Beast Walked, but after about a minute as a dingo, your eyes turned purple and you started to have a fit."

"You transitioned back just as Evie was starting to Force a walk on you, and your left hand was shuddering and flicking like you were possessed."

"Josh put you on the bed and told me to grab a sketchbook as your Dad pulled up. I've never seen anything like the way you drew. It was like you were a video on fast-forward. I'm not surprised your hand is bleeding."

I looked down at my hand. It was covered in graphite smudges, and the edge of my palm as well as the top knuckle of my middle finger were rubbed raw.

"This isn't the first time this has happened," I quietly admitted, taking a slow breath. I was stuck in this world now. There was nothing I could do. I wanted to cry. To bury myself under the covers and make the world go away. I didn't. I looked up at them instead. They looked at me with nearly identical stunned expressions. "I thought I was drawing in my sleep, like sleepwalking. So I guess I do transition, Beast Walk… whatever, in my sleep."

Moving my hand away, I took in the drawing. Anne Elliot was back. Branches still hid her face, only this time the shallow grave was guarded by a snarling, hackle-raised dog. I hissed in a slow breath. Not dog.

"Please tell me that's not me." I turned the drawing to face them.

Josh slowly shook his head with a small shrug.

Evie's voice sounded tight. "It's you."

"Oh, shit."

Chapter Twenty-Three

After everything recently, it was nice to get dressed up and go out for dinner, even if it was with my dad. The restaurant was the one Josh had taken me to, only this time I made it past the parking lot. Inside was nicer than I thought it would be, and the food at the other tables looked amazing. It was warm, and busy enough that conversation didn't quite cover the music, but not so busy you couldn't hear a conversation.

"So, what's the occasion?" I asked once we were seated. "The fact I got an A on an English assignment?"

Dad did this strange half smile, half frown thing, pulled his phone out, and scrolled through the calendar. "Did I get the date wrong? I'm sure I didn't. Nope, I'm right. This may be only the third one I've had with you, but I have the right date."

"Third what?"

"Ginny, it's the thirteenth."

I'm sure my mouth literally fell open. "Already? How did that happen?"

Dad grinned. "We live on a planet called Earth. It takes about three hundred and sixty-five days for us to travel around the sun. We call that a year. It's a rotational thing that keeps happening over and over."

I rolled my eyes at him. "You are such a dag."

"I know, but I'm a dag with an eighteen-year-old daughter. Happy birthday, sweetheart. That would have been better with a drink. Do you want a drink?"

"Can I try a cocktail?"

"Sure." He handed me the drinks menu.

"I can't believe I'm eighteen."

Last year, I couldn't wait to be eighteen. I'd be out of school and free to leave home, to get out. I wasn't counting on repeating a year of school and the whole shifter world crashing down on me. It was sad to know I was now the age where I could drink and vote, and it wasn't important. Instead, I was exhausted. I'd been Unlashing shifters all day at the Painted Serpent, and whenever I thought I'd reached the end of the line, more oozed from the woodwork. I had no idea there were so many of them. Also, nothing had mentioned how draining working with Funem-vitea was. Every shifter sapped the energy right out of me.

"I know this isn't a big party or anything, but you can still have that if you want. The property is big enough."

I nearly groaned. A big party was so the last thing I wanted. Maybe after about a week of sleep, but not right now. Not that I'd made enough friends to have a huge party anyway. Most of the people I knew here were shifters, and I was pretty sure that would raise a few eyebrows from him and more than a few tricky questions.

"I'm fine without it, though I might talk to Barbara about getting a tattoo."

I was half expecting a vehemently negative reaction, but all he did was lift his eyebrows.

"That's fine, then. Whatever you want." He smiled at the waitress, who brought a bottle of cold water and two glasses to the table, then laced his fingers together under his chin. "So, you and Josh. Are you girlfriend and boyfriend yet?"

"Dad." I rolled my eyes.

"What?"

"We're just friends."

"Yup, friends that hang out a lot. You know I don't mind him coming around, right?"

"I know that."

"But it's probably about time he and I had a serious talk."

"What sort of…. Oh hell, no, Dad, come on."

"I want to know his intentions."

"He's been the perfect gentleman. There's nothing for you to worry about. I promise."

"You do realise I was once twenty-one. Gentleman or not, I know where his thoughts are."

"Far out, Dad."

I hid my face behind the tall, thin drinks menu. He thought Josh and I were…. Oh my gosh. Heat rushed into my cheeks. This was unbelievable. I ran my eyes over ingredients for something that didn't have lime or pineapple in it.

There were times when I wondered if I should bring Dad up to speed on the whole shifter deal. After all, it was his family line that handed it to me, but each time I nearly did, I baulked. He was as normal as they came. Work, home, darts, tinkering on his car, creating stained glass works. He already had to adjust to being a full-time dad; I couldn't throw this curve ball at him. At least not yet. He was normal. He had normal. I couldn't take that away from him, no matter how much it would make my life easier and lessen my guilt.

Finally, I decided on the Bailey Mudslide and brought the menu down nearly on top of the small red box with a white ribbon. Dad's gaze was levelled at me, and I wondered how long he'd sat like that, waiting for me to notice.

"What is it?"

"Typically, with presents, you open them to find that out."

From the size and shape of the box, I was expecting some sort of jewellery, not what sat nestled in the white satin. "A key?"

"For your car. We still have to pick it up tomorrow, but I figured after five months of riding a push bike without too much complaining, you've earned it."

"A car?" I was sure I hadn't heard that correctly.

"Yes, a car."

"Are you serious?"

"Yes."

Racing around the table, I gave him a huge hug. "Thank you, Dad. Oh my gosh, thank you."

"You're welcome."

I sat back down again and pulled the key out of the box. Attached to it was a Volkswagen key ring. "A Beetle?"

"A Golf. You need something reliable."

"A Beetle isn't reliable?"

"The Golf has better handling and fuel

economy by comparison. Plus, it has airbags."

"Totally a parental response."

"There could be a good reason for that."

I grinned. I had a car. Of my own. Flipping awesome.

"You're Ginny Martin, right?" Two women approached the table. One had a transparent ghost thylacine Silver, and the older woman had a liquid silver one. I didn't know their names, although the younger of the two had short blonde hair and looked extremely familiar.

"Yes?"

"Isabelle and Anne Elliot. I didn't get to thank you the other day. I can't express how much what you did means to me."

I blinked, gripping the water glass like it was a lifeline. This was Anne Elliot. She was taller than I thought she'd be, and she had a similar hairstyle to Evie's pixie-cut blonde hair. I wasn't sure how to react. I knew she was going to die, and in the not too distant future. It took a lot of effort not to look around for the "detail" the Elders had put on her, or to react in any way that would raise suspicions.

"What did she do?" Dad asked.

My stomach hit the floor, and I played with my hair to give an excuse to put my hand up between Dad and me before giving Isabelle a pointed look. I hoped she would play along. "I designed a tattoo for her."

"And did a brilliant job. I've wanted this design for a very, very long time, but no one has been able to bring it to life, until Ginny. I'm just sorry I can't show it to you in such a public place."

Relief flooded through me. "Glad I could help."

She placed her hands on the younger woman's

shoulders. "My daughter wants one now. You might have another customer on your hands."

"If you contact the Painted Serpent, I'm sure we can make an appointment."

"Yeah, if I can talk the old fuddy-duddies of our family around." Anne crossed her arms. "You'd think I was asking to commit a crime or something."

"Anyway…" Isabelle spoke in a tone only mothers could do, the "end of discussion" tone. "I wanted to thank you. It does mean a lot."

"You're welcome."

Dad grinned as he watched them walk away. "My daughter, a town celebrity already."

"As if, Dad."

"Well, I'm proud of you."

"Thanks."

"Do you want to order now, or continue to stare at the menu for a bit longer?"

"Staring at the menu is tempting, but ordering sounds good, too."

Josh might have very bluntly pointed out I wasn't normal, but tonight I felt normal. After the Elliots left, I couldn't see another thylacine Silver, no Drawing images reared their ugly heads, and I didn't have any code to read until I was cross-eyed. Just Dad, good food, pleasant atmosphere, and a normal night. Plus, I got a car. It was the best birthday ever.

Chapter Twenty-Four

More Unlashing.

Again.

It really said something when I wished I could run away and read coded Chronicles. Dad wasn't home. He was out playing darts with Monty. I could have time and space… but, no, I was here instead. I could hear the voices from downstairs, all talking amongst themselves. Drinking coffee, eating finger food, and laughing. Oh, yes, they were having a fantastic time. They weren't the ones doing the Unlashing. At least Barbara had given me a fifteen-minute break. So here I was, sitting on the cold uncomfortable steel table, hiding.

Dad thinking I was going out with Josh bloody well helped their cause, didn't it? I could visit the Borradailes without too much suspicion, and not have to continually be called to the Painted Serpent for something that would only end up at their house anyway. I wasn't even annoyed that Barbara was right and there wasn't an actual job at the parlour for me, because the therianthrope world was taking up so much of my life.

That was what annoyed me. It wasn't even exciting like all that supernatural stuff on TV. It was boring. Reading. Long discussions with Lori, Miriam, and Evie about Lashing and Unlashing. Going around and around in circles about government conspiracy theories and the demise of therianthropes. If I heard one more of Miriam's "the government is out to kill us" speeches, I was sure I was going to scream. Recording all the Elder's files into the Chronicles, and the same with these murder investigations. Unlashing. Yes, I wanted normal. Yes, this was becoming soul-numbingly normal. But normal didn't mean suddenly becoming a flipping beck-and-call admin officer, for Pete's sake.

Leaning my head back against the wall, I passed my eyes over the cluttered space across the opposite side of the attic, where all the files, boards, timelines, and maps were set up. Chocolate biscuits and coffee downstairs worked like magic at clearing this room. I was finally on my own for a few minutes. The tension over on that side in the last week was building like a tidal wave, and I was glad they didn't want me to be a part of the murder mystery. Hopefully, I'd be well out of the way when it all came crashing down. But I couldn't help feeling their sickening anticipation. Anne Elliot was still alive, and it was already the 20th of May without a body. Eight to ten days after the regular timeline. Either a body had yet to be found, or Anne was still the target and the timeline had changed. I didn't want to voice the third option that spun in my head like a small cyclone—that Anne was still to be a victim, just not for months, yet. The Elders didn't need that option unleashed on them when they were all wound up like this. One of them was likely to explode.

The melody of my phone went off, and I fished it out of my bag, glancing briefly at the display.

"Hi, Evie."

"Where are you?"

I frowned and jumped off the table, reacting to her voice. Evie sounded freaked out. "In the Borradailes' attic. Why?"

"I've had a terrible premonition. The death hand dealt, drawn from the font of knowledge. The loss of one, the thylacine and canis lupus combined."

I ran the words over in my head. The last part of that sent a cold trickle of dread down my spine. "You don't know for sure what that means."

"No, I don't know, but I think you're in danger."

"It certainly doesn't sound healthy." I leaned against the door. "If your premonitions work the way mine do, you have no way of telling—"

"With the murders, do you really want to take that chance?"

"Calm down. Okay? You need to slow down. Take it easy. One step at a time. I know they can get a little freaky sometimes, but premonitions aren't the whole story. Remember that."

"I know that, but you also drew you, transitioned at the crime scene, remember? Has Josh looked at that drawing?"

"He's seen it, same as you."

"No, I mean has he *looked* at it. Really studied it. For clues and details that could be important."

"I don't know. Probably not."

"Get him to look at the sketch. Now."

"That's a little hard at the moment. He went to play darts with his Dad. To get away from the boredom of this place, no doubt. Not that I blame him. If I wouldn't be gate crashing a boys' night, I probably would have joined him. It totally blew my cover, though. I had to say I was coming here to help Barbara with some drawings."

"Ginny, focus. Where's the sketchbook?"

I rubbed my face, trying to think. "I'm not sure. I think it's in my room. I have sketchbooks all over the place these days. Some are here, some are in my room, and one or two are in the dungeon."

"Have a look there and get back to me. In the meantime, I'm heading to your place to find it. We need to have Josh look at it."

"Are you sure you want to be this dramatic?"

"I'd rather be overdramatic for a false alarm than be under-dramatic and have the 'death hand dealt,' if it's all the same to you."

"You can't go to my place. No one will be home. Dad's playing darts, too."

"I'll break in if I have to."

"Evie…."

"What?"

I sighed. I was sure she was overreacting, but, apparently, a herd of wild bulls wasn't going to stop her at this point. "What exactly are you going to do with the book once you've got it?"

"Head over to the Borradailes and wait for him."

"Geez, can you at least wait until I check here?"

"I'm getting in the car now, Ginny."

A different dread slashed through my stomach at her words. "Not talking to me on the phone, you're not.

"Do you have the sketchbook or not?" I heard a door opening at her end.

"Don't start that car, Evie." My fist clenched as my stomach lurched into my throat, frantically hoping I wouldn't hear the engine of her car. I struggled to get the words out. "Do not use the phone and drive, okay? Ever."

"I'm not driving. I'm sitting in my driveway."

"Promise?"

"I promise. I'm just sitting here."

"Okay." It took me a few seconds to calm down and start pulling the sketchbook from my bag.

"Ginny?"

"I'm looking, I'm looking." I remembered the sketchbook was the one with the half-drawn night sky with fireworks. The image went from fully drawn and coloured, transitioning to merely drawn, to fading, to sketched, and then finally to a blank page, with a hand holding a red pencil hovered over it all. "I can't do this holding the phone."

"I'm going to your place."

I sighed. "Don't be silly. I'll bring it here tomorrow. He can look at it then."

"You can meet me there, or I can break in. Your choice."

"You're mad. You know that, don't you?"

"Concerned for your safety."

"One night isn't going to—" I heard her car engine. "Evie."

"I'm hanging up and heading to your place."

"Wait. Far out. You're crazy. Let me check here. If it's not here, I'll head home. Don't waste petrol."

"Have you got a spare key?"

"What?"

"Your house. Is there a spare key outside or something?"

"Yes, but—"

"Good. Text me with the location of the key. This can't wait, Ginny. He needs to look at it tonight."

"Evie…."

All I got was dead air.

"Fantastic. Just fuc—"

"What's up?" Barbara appeared at the doorway.

"Evie's lost it."

"Lost what?"

"Everything. The plot. Her mind." I started going through the sketchbooks. Knowing my luck, it would be the last one I picked up, but at least then everything could calm down.

Barbara put a hand on my arm. "What's going on?"

"Did Josh happen to mention he's my Interpreter?"

"He did mention something about that, why?"

"Evie's had a premonition. We need him to look at one of my drawings."

"And?"

"She wants him to do it today. Now."

"He won't be back from playing darts for another two hours."

"I know. I told Evie that."

"I'm sure it can wait until tomorrow."

"Preaching to the choir here," I muttered. "Obviously, when she has a bee in her bonnet, there's no stopping her. Great, it's not here."

"It has to wait at least until you've Unlashed—"

"It's about the murders. At least she thinks so."

Barbara drew her breath in on a hiss and lowered her voice. "I can't let you do a runner. Those therianthropes down there know nothing about the murders, and I'd like to keep it that way. Finish Unlashing them, which will be, what? Half an hour, tops? Then we can discuss this like calm, rational people. Deal?"

I closed the third and final sketchbook I had in my bag. "Deal. But I have to make one call first."

"Okay. They're ready for you down there, by the way."

"I won't be a sec."

Pushing my fringe back, I sighed as I stared blindly at the map across the room. The little red dots and their bits of string nearly merging into one and bleeding across the paper when I rubbed my face. Well, at least Evie's little drama was more exciting than normal. I laughed bitterly as I sent her a text I hoped like hell she wouldn't read until she stopped driving. Normal? Yeah, right.

I couldn't rush the Unlashing. Most of it was done by feel, and I had to move carefully to keep the tingles inside my fists. Barbara was nearly bang on the money with the time. Twenty-six minutes later, the fourth shifter was finally Unlashed, but it was another fifteen minutes or so before she could convince them to leave. They were Beast Walking all over the place, and if I got one more hug, I was going to lose it.

"Okay." She locked the front door and turned back to me. "Spill."

It took me a second to realise she meant I needed to tell the Elders. Crossing my arms, I repeated the whole "Evie's insisting Josh looks at the drawing" story.

Cornelia glanced at her watch. "The boys will be home in about an hour. Call her and tell her to meet us here, and let your dad know we've invited you to dinner."

"You know this is probably a false alarm, right?" I spoke as I dialled. She should have reached my place by now.

Barbara nodded. "Perhaps. After all, we've reached the twentieth without a body being found, and Anne Elliot is still alive and well."

Yeah, and I knew how relaxed that was making everyone. I reached Evie's voicemail. Hanging up, I tried again with the same result.

"I'm going to head on out to the house. She might not be able find the key. We'll head back as soon as we have the book."

Chapter Twenty-Five

Pulling up at the house, I saw Evie's car, but no Evie. Obviously, she was inside. Since I wasn't going to be here long, I parked next to her. Hugging my jacket around me against the cold, I ran around to the back door. It was locked. For a second, I stared at my hand on the knob stupidly before knocking on the door.

"Evie?"

No answer. I peered inside, not seeing any movement.

"Evie? Open up. It's Ginny." I knocked again.

Fan-bloody-tastic. If she was down in the dungeon, she would never hear me, but she still should have seen me come down the drive. It was only then I remembered Evie didn't know about the security system down there. She wouldn't have known what the pings meant.

Opening the woodshed door, I reached for the hook hidden by the handtowel.

No key.

Great.

Muttering to myself, I dashed back to the car and grabbed the garage remote. I didn't know anything about security systems and what not, but the next thing I was doing was getting an extra camera for the front door, so you could see someone standing there. Getting that past Dad was another problem, but I was sure I'd work it out.

Somehow.

Ducking under the door, I set it back down as I hit the light switch. At least it was warmer in here. I started to go around Dad's workbench, but then had to backtrack so I didn't walk into his car, and went around the other side, where my car was now normally parked. Opening the kitchen door, I stopped and turned slowly.

Dad's car?

That was odd. I could only guess someone else had picked him up for darts.

"Hello?" I called out as I entered the house. "Evie?"

No one answered. There was no one in the kitchen or lounge room or the bathroom. I even checked Dad's room, because I happened to be going past. All empty.

In my room, my sketchbooks had been moved. Apparently, Evie hadn't found the one with the drawing, which meant there was only one place she could be. As I entered the passage behind my wardrobe, my nose twitched. The air smelled different. The lights were on and cast an orange glow in the passage. It was odd being able to see without a torch. Much better. I might leave the lights on from now on.

"Did you find it?" I asked as I stepped into the room. For a second, what I saw didn't register, and when it did, I stopped dead in my tracks. "Far out."

The room was empty of people but in complete shambles. It was an absolute mess. It looked like it had been ransacked. The table was on its side, books were everywhere, the glass in the shelves was shattered, and there was stuff scattered all over the place.

Any normal person when faced with this would immediately turn around and call the cops. That's what my first reaction was, and I had already dialled the second 0 towards 000, when it hit me exactly where I was standing.

I hung up. I couldn't bring the cops here. I froze, undecided. I had no idea what to do. Did I call the Elders? Did I look around for myself? Did I wait around long enough for whoever did this to come back?

Still, without knowing what the best course of action was, I took a cautious step forward, hoping like hell I wasn't going to trip over something nasty. Like a body. My foot kicked something that gave off a dull metallic clink. Frowning, I bent to pick up the object that couldn't be real.

"A bullet. What the…?"

A handful of bullets were strewn around an open and upside-down metal box. It was one of the metal boxes Josh and I couldn't open. Reaching for it, I tilted it the right way up and held it in my hands. In its depths was a shaped cavity in firm foam and bullets still snug in the circular holes riddled along the edge of the foam. I dropped the box and searched the immediate vicinity. The dungeon apparently had a shitload of guns, and one was missing.

"Shit."

Okay, next step. I got the hell out of here. I wasn't a blonde in a horror movie. It would take more than a cordless phone to strangle me. As I stood up, the centre of the tapestry billowed out like a bubble on water and I froze, nearly having a heart attack, until it settled back into place as a gust of frigid air hit me. No other movement came from behind it. My heart was pounding in my head and I struggled to get air through my suddenly closed throat.

"Move, damn it," I hissed at myself.

I moved. In the wrong direction. It didn't matter that my head was flashing all the killer scenes from all the horror movies I'd ever seen. My feet took me, creeping carefully, across the mess, and a shaking hand flicked the switch to move the heavy fabric. My heart was racing so fast I nearly couldn't hear the mechanical drone as the tapestry revealed the wall behind it… and the open door.

After about three seconds, I finally coordinated my body back near the entrance so I could get reception on my phone. I rang Barbara and had to leave a message. I rang Cornelia next, but she didn't answer. Running out of options, I dialled Josh. There was no ring tone. Looking at the screen, I saw it hadn't connected. I tried again with the same result. I didn't have anyone else's number. We didn't have a house phone, and I was pretty sure Dad would have taken his with him.

My body started to shake uncontrollably. I had no clue what to do. I couldn't process anything other than this was wrong. So very wrong. A freezing blast of air whipped through the room, riffling papers and tinkling broken glass, and suddenly I didn't have to decide anything. My beast hit me full force and the vertigo turned into a world of black and white with the scent of Evie and blood on the wind.

Chasing the wind, I ran from the room along the rich earth cavern, out into the twilight. The scent I was seeking only came in puffs along the cold edge of the breeze. I waited out a few breeze changes then turned into the direction it came from most often. I caught every motion. Leaves, grass, birds, a wallaby, but I didn't let it distract me. I needed to find the Seer before the blood turned cold on the wind. More than her scent, I could feel her. An agonising tension in my head.

Danger.

Reaching the top of the rise, the wind blew my fur hard against my body, and I heard a loud, echoed thunder that brought with it a hot, sharp burn on the breeze and flung the birds into the sky. I froze. I didn't know what it was or where it came from. Along the pull at my stomach, I felt the awareness of the human bringing a concept into my head.

Gun.

The concept bristled the hair on my back and I ran in the direction of the blood scent. The sharp burn of 'gun' nearly overpowered it. The breeze changed directions and under the gun and blood were more scents. Many more. Mingled and confusing. I sniffed the wind again. Another scent. Familiar and wrong.

It was stronger now. Slowing, I stalked. Noticing and dismissing the ordinary. Then through the crossed branches, I saw the movement of men.

"What the hell are you doing? You shot her."

"They'll come now. They won't be able to help themselves."

"Who will come? You said this was the last one. It's over. Take her and go."

The scent of the Seer came with the burning scent of blood. I moved closer and eased past the trees to where the scent was strongest. The Seer was on the ground, the muddied black of blood glistening on her body and pooling on the dirt. I had to protect the Seer at all costs.

With a growl, I lunged. Soft man flesh would be easy to tear apart. He turned, bringing his hand around. I would reach him first. Triumph was mine. Seconds before my teeth sank into the tender flesh, my human burst through and the world blurred, becoming blinding colours as I stumbled to a stop.

"Dad?"

Chapter Twenty-Six

"Dad?"

My attention was pulled across the clearing to where my gasp was repeated in a slow drawl. "Well, now, isn't that interesting?"

"Ginny?" Dad's voice was barely a whisper, but the horror in his eyes screamed far too loud. "No."

"This does change some things, now, doesn't it?"

A chorus of cold, metallic clicks echoed around us and Dad spun as if yanked by a string, putting himself directly in front of me. It took a few seconds to register the two glossy black SUVs and the three men in suits, all holding guns.

"You have what you want, Anderson. We had a deal. Now get off my land."

"Not yet, I don't. Although, this does make a nice consolation prize."

"You wanted the girl with the purple eyes. You have her. Now go."

The ferocious need to protect rushed at me

from my beast and blocked out the fear and the confusion.

Evie.

I spun, the confronting sight dropped me to my knees. Blood spilled through her fingers as she clutched her stomach. She was still alive, curled in pain, and lying in a shallow ditch half hidden by branches.

It had never been Anne Elliot.

She was still alive. I had time. I could save her. My hand went for my phone, but a hard pull yanked me to my feet and I felt something cold against my head.

"Leave her alone."

Dad's words held more desperation than authority, and he had his own suit with a gun to deal with. They half dragged, half pushed us across the clearing, closer to the cars.

"She's bleeding to death. You have to save her."

The cold smile didn't reach Anderson's eyes, and it sent icicles of fear stabbing through me. He was going to let her die.

Calmly, he holstered his gun and casually clasped his hands in front of him. They were eerily pale against his dark suit in the twilight. "You and I are going to have a little conversation."

"Go to hell."

His pleasant laugh rasped over my nerves and he turned to Dad. "She has spunk. I like spunk."

"She has nothing to do with this, Anderson. This is between you and me."

"Now, no longer true. So, unless you'd like to see a bullet between those pretty blue eyes, I suggest one of you explains how *your daughter* morphed from a dog."

Dread slammed into me like a cold wave. I was supposed to protect therianthropes, and instead I'd busted their world right out into the open. Blindly, I'd shifted in front of humans, and I had no idea how to stuff the genie back into the bottle. I couldn't even pretend that I hadn't. Just as dread was twisting into panic in the silence, an almost audible clicking sounded in my head. The SUVs, which I could now see, held cages in the back. The calm question. The knowledge of what purple eyes meant. Anderson already knew. Fear still bubbled under the surface, but the dread ebbed away. I had a focus now. I had to find out how much he knew.

"I didn't morph from a dog."

"Well, it certainly wasn't from a thylacine."

Swallowing hard, I tried to ignore the two guns pointed at us, and hoped like hell my voice wouldn't come out in a squeak. "A conversation goes both ways, Mr Anderson, and it's not every day I walk through my backyard to find strange cars, men in suits, and guns."

Even I could hear the tremble in my words, but this time his smile had a hint of genuine warmth. It was almost more frightening than his cold smile.

"It would appear your father owes you an explanation."

The oily slide of his words over my skin made me think of those bad guys in movies that told the good guys the plan, then designed a way for the good guys to die with enough time to escape and save the world. It gave me a trickle of hope.

"Ginny…." Dad's voice trailed off, and Anderson's smile broadened.

Reaching into his jacket, Anderson pulled out a

little black folder. Opening it, he revealed a circular badge, all gold, with an image of Australia, set atop the Australian coat of arms, and topped with a crown. Stamped across the golden country were the letters TICA.

"TICA?"

"Therianthrope Investigation and Containment Agency."

Agency? There was a whole agency? Dread danced back with heavy lead feet as I registered the "containment" part of the name. Guns, cages, and they now knew I was a therianthrope. My sudden shaking had nothing to do with the cold.

"Are you, like, a secret government agent?"

Anderson didn't even blink. "You watch too much American TV. Australia doesn't have agents. We have officers. As for the secret... well, we don't show up in the Australian Government Directory."

"And you're in our backyard, because...?"

My words might have been casual, but I knew by the return of the cold smile Anderson could smell the fear rolling off me in waves.

"Because, until five minutes ago, when you showed your true nature, your father was working for us."

"This is getting out of hand. I don't know what is going on here, but Ginny is not... she's not.... It's impossible."

"Impossible?" Anderson's smile faded and his face became... pleasant.

That lack of emotion was far more terrifying than anything I'd ever experienced. I struggled against the suit who held me as Anderson opened a car door and reached inside, pulling out a small silver case.

"Twenty-five out of twenty-five, and a Seer. You did seem too good to be true, Doherty."

Twenty-five. The number echoed in my mind as the wall of photos from the Borradailes' attic flashed in my head.

"Dad?"

Anderson set the case on the front of the car and withdrew a tiny glass jar and a syringe.

"Impossible to have a hundred percent therianthrope strike rate without an advantageous edge, wouldn't you say?"

The needle of the syringe went into the lid of the small upside-down jar, and Anderson withdrew a small amount of clear liquid.

"This is G-23, a rather benign name for a chemical compound that has the most amazing effect on therianthropes. Once injected, it forces them to shift, revealing themselves. The only thing is, we haven't quite perfected the formula. Once they shift back to human form, well, they die. Gruesomely. It takes a few days, but in the end.... The good news: it has no effect on humans. Completely harmless. Let's test your impossibility theory, shall we?"

He flicked the syringe and advanced.

Chapter Twenty-Seven

I couldn't break free. The suit's grip was far too strong. No amount of kicking, throwing myself around, or wriggling made him release his hold. He wrapped a steel band of an arm around me and gripped tighter, holding me immobile.

Anderson closed the gap and yanked the various layers of collars aside to expose my neck. A snarling yell came from my left, and suddenly Anderson was down in a surged flurry of movement. Dad had broken free and grappled with him, slamming his fist into the officer's face with a sound that was nothing like it was in the movies. It was harsher and dulled, like an axe into wood. In a frantic surge, Anderson was on top and managed to swing his fist, connecting with Dad's shoulder before he was under him again. Dad landed more blows. After the third, Anderson didn't move. Breathing heavily, Dad stayed where he was for a long moment before he scrambled to his feet.

"Don't think you can outrun a bullet, Doherty." The suit's breath was hot on my cheek as Dad swayed. His eyes locked with mine were full of desperation. He tensed and I knew. My father was going to try to run directly into a loaded gun to save me.

A low growl rumbled around us with the intensity of a small engine, while hissing howls wailed into the cold air like banshees, freezing the blood in my veins. The gun's aim flew from my head to the advancing hoard of thylacine and devils. They circled the vehicles and officers, hackles raised, anger and determination radiating in waves. Even the human Silvers seemed seconds from attacking.

My knees gave way in relief and I dropped to the ground, the suit apparently unable to hold my full weight. He pointed the gun from one shifter to the next, unloading six bullets into howls and sounds of pain before the hoards descended, a crashing wave that nearly took me with it. The officer bolted for the car, scrabbling for the door handle behind him. He should have known better. Origin thylacine and devils would have had no chance at getting in the car once he was inside, but he wasn't dealing with them. They surrounded Anderson and the others, and I saw a few shift to human form to yank the cages from the cars.

I crawled the few meters to where Dad had fallen to his knees, grabbing his shoulder.

He clutched me in a hug for a few seconds before releasing me. He was shaking even more than I was.

"Ginny, are you okay?"

"Yeah, you?"

"Few bruises." He waved an unsteady hand across the clearing. "Evie."

Scrambling to my feet, I ran across to her, skidding down into the mud as I landed on my knees. Her eyes were open, staring blankly into the overcast sky, and she wasn't moving.

"Evie, no."

I didn't know what to do. In movies, they always checked for a pulse somewhere on the neck, but I didn't know how to do that. I didn't know what I was feeling for or where to put my fingers.

"Ginny, what happened?"

A strong hand grabbed my jacket and moved me aside. Scott knelt where I had been. Another tap on the shoulder moved me further away as Cornelia knelt beside him.

"She's been shot."

He checked her pulse then both of them started CPR.

"Is she going to be okay?" My beast was still sending the need to protect down the Funem-vitea, but it was also starting to whimper.

"I don't know," Scott muttered.

"We need to call an ambulance."

"We've got it, Ginny," Cornelia told me. "I need you to find Barbara. You need to give her a rundown on what happened here. Can you do that?"

"I...." I couldn't think. I couldn't move.

"Ginny. She's going to be okay. We're here now."

I swallowed and nodded. It wasn't easy when their Silvers were staring at Evie with intense concentration, but I nodded again and moved. They needed room and I was only in the way.

Barbara.

I had to find Barbara. Give her a rundown. Yes. The Elders needed to know what happened. They would make it right. They would know what to do.

Standing, I stumbled three steps, and came to a dead stand-still. There was movement everywhere. Thylacine, devils, Silvers, and humans. There was a mob swarming like bees around the vehicles and a suit raging on the inside of a cage. It wasn't the movement that caught me like a deer in headlights. It was the stillness. The stillness of the dingo, collapsed, near the cars, where Dad had been. Very, very still.

"Dad!"

My own cry moved my feet, and I dodged movement and motion to reach him. It took forever. The distance between us wasn't getting any shorter. Then in a heartbeat, I was at his side, my hands searching his fur for movement. I felt it; he breathed.

With a sob, I buried my head in his side. Everything was too much. The fear, the adrenaline, the mess.

"It's over now," I whispered into his fur, moving closer to wrap my arms around him. "It's...."

Something dug into my knee, and I pulled it out from under me. It was the syringe. Anderson must have dropped it. I had to find the case and put it away safely. It was far too dangerous out here in the open with so many therianthropes. That's when I noticed the plunger. It wasn't pulled back with liquid sloshing in the tube. The plunger was depressed the entire way down.

Empty.

"No," I breathed, seeing the fight again in my mind. Anderson had landed that one fist. Into Dad's shoulder. A sideways slam. This time, my scream

was pulled out from somewhere down in my
shattered soul.

"Dad!"

Chapter Twenty-Eight

A dingo's head in a woman's lap, another drawing prediction fulfilled. It didn't matter that the dingo was my father, my hand gently stroking the short sandy fur, teasing the dappled sunlight into a small wave of motion. Josh's legs were warm against my right side, but I could tell from his stillness and breathing he'd finally fallen asleep up on the sofa behind me. To the left, Barbara and Cornelia spoke in low voices in the kitchen. Most of the shifters had left hours ago, and I'd lost track of who was still in the house.

My eyes were gritty, and I could feel a headache building. Each blink was a sweet siren song to sleep, but I couldn't give in. Not yet.

It was a relief to hear the front door open and have something to focus on, even if apprehension clawed closely behind. Nothing that had come through that front door had been any release from the draining merry-go-round. I could hear footsteps along the short hallway before Miriam appeared. She looked as bad as I felt. Her braid was loose and a halo of grey hair surrounded her head as though she'd spent a lot of the night running her hands through it. Dark circles under her eyes made her face age twenty years, but that could have also been because her face was so pale.

"She's out of surgery and currently stable." She held up her phone as she faltered to a halt just inside the lounge room. "Still in ICU."

"You can go to the hospital, Miriam." Cornelia came out of the kitchen to stand beside her. "We're fine here. You don't need to be here when David wakes."

Shaking her head, Miriam sat on Dad's La-Z-Boy and pulled her laptop onto her lap, immediately burying herself in whatever she was typing. "I need to keep busy."

Having failed with Miriam, Cornelia turned to me. "Ginny, you should get some sleep. We can watch him."

It took too much effort to speak, so I just shook my head.

"You're practically zombies, both of you." Barbara crossed her arms behind her mother. "Sacrificing sleep doesn't make you heroic, you know? It just makes you unable to function."

"And when, exactly, did you sleep?" Josh's voice was a low rasp from behind me.

I tilted my head up to the right and saw that he hadn't bothered to open his eyes.

"I got a few hours, which is more than I can say for all of you."

With effort, I tilted my head forward again, hoping they weren't going to start an argument. I didn't have the energy for that.

"I think I might have an answer."

This time, my head tilted to the left and brought Miriam into view, but I couldn't make sense of her announcement.

"Answer to what?" Cornelia prompted when Miriam didn't continue.

"In 1950, Alice White married Origin human Graham Doherty. Their son, Andrew, married Lynn Foster. And that explains it."

My frown flared my headache but didn't help to clear up the befuddled confusion.

Barbara bent down at Miriam's side, the sun pouring in through the open windows reflecting off the orange of her dress and causing an orange glow around the room while she read whatever was on the screen. "It's the right spelling and he's the right age."

"Look at the marriage certificate." Miriam pointed. "Born in Queenstown, Tasmania."

"It does make sense. And look at this. Graham, Andrew, David. Same line."

Now Cornelia was getting in on the whole group of mysterious understanding.

"And we didn't see it before, because we were looking down his paternal line to find Rachel, not the maternal." Barbara added.

"What's going on?" I was half expecting them to pull out badges and organise a secret handshake.

"Graham is the name of Rachel's son. The one who moved to Queensland in 1944," Barbara told me.

Josh nudged me gently with his leg. "It explains why you're a therianthrope."

"It takes three generations for therianthropes bloodlines to form or to be extinguished," Cornelia added.

"Alice came from a pure bloodline, so even married to a human, she had a good chance for her children to continue the line. Andrew did, and he married a pure bloodline, too. David, your father, is a pureblood canis lupus therianthrope, as he is the third generation of unions with therianthropes, and he had you."

"Oh." I blinked as I struggled to make Miriam's explanation more than a jumble of words. "So it's all Graham's fault."

There was a heartbeat of silence then Barbara snorted. That started Josh with a few puffed chuckles. Cornelia followed with low giggles, and that set me off. It wasn't all that funny, but the laughter fed off our overstressed, adrenaline-drained exhaustion, and it became hysterical. When it settled, one of us would snicker, and then we were in for another round. Caught in the hysteria, I missed the movement from my lap. In a clumsy, uncoordinated motion, Dad stumbled to his feet.

"Ginny." Josh leaned forward, watching him.

I'd never deliberately shifted before, and for a moment I hovered between "I have to shift" and "oh hell, what do I do?" before my beast rushed me headlong into black-and-white vision and far too many scents. For the first time, I felt the "whoa" feeling of a sudden drop before my human settled herself somewhere behind my bellybutton.

"It's okay." I felt a lash of surprise from my human as I used body language and position to communicate, and not barks as I felt she expected. The concepts still came across loud and clear. Ignoring her, I focused on Dad. I kept still, expecting him to freak out, and not knowing what to do if he did.

"We're safe."

"Ginny? What…?"

"We're in the house, and the Elders have dealt with the government people."

"Who? How?"

I decided to focus on what I thought was important. "I don't know. I was here with you, dreading you'd shift before Miriam could Lash you."

His eyes flicked, and I could tell he was attempting to make sense of that.

"You can't be human again. If you shift out of Beast Walk, you'll die. Anderson pumped you full of that G-13 shit. Miriam tied you off, so you shouldn't be able to shift back. It's called Lashing. She even did it twice, which we hope will stop you from instinctively shifting like the thylacine used to."

Now, his deep amber eyes were locked on me. "How long have you known?"

Slowly, I lifted my head. I thought he'd show some sort of shocked reaction; his calm was odd. "Which part? That ther… shifters exist? Three months. That I'm a shifter? About a month. That you're a shifter? Yesterday, which incidentally is when I found out about a secret government agency that doesn't appear to like our kind very much."

I felt a tremor from my human at the words 'our kind' but tried not to show it. This wasn't the time to show weakness. My father was moving smoothly and showed no signs of any ill effects. I hid my concern for his wellbeing behind a stern expression. I wanted answers.

"You endangered our Seer."

"I was protecting you."

"Protecting me? By handing our Seer over to them?"

He stood his ground for a moment then dropped his shoulders. "I didn't know she was the Seer until she was shot."

"You knew about her purple eyes."

"Because I'd seen them change colour. Anderson wanted the girl with the purple eyes. I wasn't about to give them you."

"Why would you give them anyone? Why were you involved with them in the first place?"

My attention moved away briefly as the older Seer moved into my line of vision. She was intently watching something across the room. When I returned my gaze to my father, his chest had dropped nearly to the ground and he'd turned his head toward the window, staring at it as if it held all the answers he needed.

"They're government officers. Like the police. They were supposed to be the good guys."

I blinked, struggling to understand his words. They felt familiar, but I couldn't quite grasp them.

Government.

Police.

A nudge from my human brought the concepts into my mind, and I frowned. I knew those. I could see them. Anderson. Yes. I didn't know why they had slipped from my mind, but I could remember them now.

"A ranger's salary isn't all it's cracked up to be. They wanted names. I gave them. I didn't know they were killing them. At least not until the hikers found Victor Borradaile."

"Borradaile is the same last name as your work colleague and dart buddy. That didn't register with you?" I sat up with my legs stretched out straight.

"It was just a name."

"And how did you know the others?"

"I read them. This house has a vault, and it is filled with an entire history of therianthropes."

I stared at him, the sun glinting off his pale fur almost a glare in my eyes. "How did you read the code?"

His head swung slowly, turning from the window to look intently at me. "You found the vault?"

"Yes."

"That explains why things moved. I should have guessed."

"We could have saved a lot of heartache if you'd told me about the dungeon and the Chronicles in the first place, and the fact you knew about it."

"'Hi, honey, I'm not crazy, but there are people who can turn into animals and we have an entire secret vault under the house filled with coded records.' I'm sure that conversation would have worked if you weren't already moonlighting with a secret double life—which I knew nothing about, by the way."

"I didn't want to suck you into this world, and I didn't know how to tell you about it, either."

"Well, I'm sucked into it now. What did you say Miriam did?"

I frowned. Miriam? Yes, the Seer. "Lashed you. Double Lashed, actually, to be on the safe side."

"And this stops me from shifting back. To human."

"Lashing stops you from shifting back to human at will, but it doesn't stop the flight-or-fight response that can cause a shift. So, double Lashing."

He lowered himself down with a thump and placed his head on his paws. "To be on the safe side. Yeah, I've got it."

"Dad, you heard Anderson. We can't risk you shifting—"

"I know, sweetheart. It doesn't make it any easier."

"You're taking it better than I thought you would."

"It's better than I deserve."

"What?"

"It's my fault that dozens of people died. I should be given the death penalty. Locked up at the very least. If this is to be my prison, then so be it."

The finality in his tone pierced my heart. "Dad, it's not your fault."

He didn't say anything, didn't even look in my direction.

"Dad."

I couldn't think of what else to say as his gaze returned to the window. Moving backward, I shifted as I stood and found the three of them all watching me. The lounge room felt claustrophobic and there wasn't enough air. Without thinking about it, I shifted again and escaped through the open back door. The bright sunshine was warm on my back as I ran. I couldn't run fast enough. I was trapped.

My father.

My world.

My life.

Everything spun in a whirlpool. I would never be free. It had pulled me down and it would never let me go. It would never be over.

I stopped running. I had nowhere to go. Nowhere to escape to. My chest heaved as I dragged cold air into my lungs. It grated over my throat as I panted, but it wasn't as painful as the hollow emptiness inside.

Catching a familiar scent on the breeze, I didn't turn, even as I heard a nearly silent rustle behind me. I shifted instead, watching the approaching thylacine do the same.

Josh didn't say anything. His eyes watched the tears as they started to fall down my cheeks, and he simply closed the gap between us, wrapping his arms around me as I finally gave in.

Chapter Twenty-Nine

The ratchet of the packing tape dispenser nearly covered the sound of the burbling engine approaching the house. Dad lifted his head then leaped lightly off the sofa.

"Yeah, yeah. I hear it." Slapping the tape against the top of the box, I left the packing to open the front door as the black bike slowed to a stop in the driveway. With an effortless swing that definitely showed his jean-clad backside to the best advantage, Josh got off the bike and removed his helmet, shaking his head to settle his hair.

"Hey," I called out.

"Hey." He lifted his chin in greeting. "How are you holding up?"

"As well as can be expected, I suppose."

Setting the helmet on the handlebars, he stepped up onto the front porch, using a hand to further shake out his hair. It fell to both sides of his face.

"So," he said, crossing his arms.

"So?"

"I had an interesting conversation with my parents."

I held my breath then stepped back to let him into the house. Like pulling a Band-Aid off, this was better done quickly. No use in dragging it out.

He closed the door behind us then stopped at the sight of the boxes in the lounge room.

"So it is true. When *exactly* were you going to tell me you were leaving?"

"I haven't, *exactly*…" I stressed the word, putting the same emphasis he had put on it. "…had the chance."

"But you managed to tell the Elders."

"I have a responsibility to them, Josh. It's something they need to know."

"And I don't?"

"It's different."

"Why?"

I grabbed the tape dispenser to give myself something to do then stared down at it in my hands.

"Scott had me report Dad as a missing person, and I had to tell Mum. So, she'll be here next week to take me back to Townsville. I'll be finishing the school year there."

"You're running away."

My head shot up at the deep-toned accusation. "I am not running away."

He took a step closer, flinging his hand to indicate the boxes. "Then why leave? You can finish the school year here."

"Have you forgotten about Anderson and the rest of TICA? They know where I live."

"The Elders—"

"Have put their detail on me, I know. But how long do you think they can keep that up? Forever?

Not likely. This is something I have to do, Josh."

"Why?"

"What do you mean, why?"

"Why do you have to go back to Townsville?"

"I told you. Mum is—"

"You're eighteen."

I crossed my arms, bumping the dispenser on my bicep. "Yeah, so?"

"Legally, you don't have to go back to your mother."

"I have to start somewhere."

That made him blink, which was followed by a frown and a slow crossing of his arms. "Start? Start what?"

"Looking for the other therath…. Far out, you'd think I'd be able to say that word by now."

"Shifters." Josh slowly uncrossed his arms. "You're looking for the other therianthropes?"

"Yeah." I placed the dispenser on the top of the box. I was starting to feel silly holding it. "The kangaroos and the flying foxes and the rest. Didn't your parents tell you that?"

Hooking his thumbs into the pockets of his jeans, he gave a sheepish grin. "I may have left before they got that far."

"If we exist, they have to exist. They were on the Lashing imagery. It makes sense. You saw what we were capable of when we banded together, and that was only three species. There's at least four more out there somewhere, Josh. I need to find them. Miriam said that Seers will find other Seers; it's like an instinct. That's how they found me, and Lori. I can find them. At least, I have to try. Working together, we've a better chance at putting a stop to Anderson and his goons." I tilted my head at him. "If you didn't know that, why did you think I was leaving?"

He gave a spot of grey carpet his full attention for a long moment before he answered. "You want normal. Townsville is normal."

I smiled at the irony of his words.

"Square peg, round hole. Remember? This world…" I circled my finger to indicate Dad, him, me, and the rest of it all, even as the twinge of empty hollowness still echoed. "The shifters and codes and the ton of Latin words, this is my new normal. And, yes, I'm still getting used to that, and yes, it's not easy, but this is my world now. TICA doesn't get to take that away from me. Not if I can help it."

"You can still do all that from Tasmania. You don't have to leave."

I took a slow, deep breath and gave that grey carpet some attention of my own. It was going to start getting a complex soon.

"You sound like a broken record, Josh. Anderson and the rest of them, the Elders might not want to tell me how they made them apparently disappear, but they're a good reason to leave. I'd need a pretty compelling reason to stay with that hanging over my head."

He was quiet long enough that I glanced up to see what his silent reaction was. In that moment, he stepped closer and placed a gentle hand along the side of my jaw. His hair tickled my cheek as he lowered his head before my brain figured it out in the second his lips touched mine. For about a heartbeat, I didn't know how to react before it just seemed right to place my hand on his chest and tilt my head. His breath was warm, even as the touch of his tongue made me shiver. As his arm went around my waist to pull me closer, I heard a low growl from below us. Without wanting to, my head pulled back as I tried to identify the sound. Practically in unison, both Josh and I looked down at Dad. It was eerie how he made that tilt of his head look disapprovingly human.

"Parental overbearing, much," I muttered. "You're just mad because you haven't had that talk with Josh you wanted."

"What talk?"

"You know, father to potential boyfriend."

Josh's eyes widened, and a slow smile pulled at his lips as he leaned closer again. "Yeah, good luck with that."

The second kiss was even better than the first, but it ended in the same way. Pulling back, I laughed as Dad's growl increased in intensity, like someone revving a throttle. Biting my lip, I let Josh's hand slip down my shoulder to hold my hand as he pulled back.

"This doesn't change things, you know. I'm still leaving."

Josh's eyebrows lifted for a second before he gave a slow nod. "Then I'm coming with you."

"Whoa." I took a step back and stared at him. "Don't you think that's a bit hasty?"

His hand hung empty in the air for a moment before he shook his head and slid his thumbs back into the pockets of his jeans. "I'm your interpreter. You may need me."

I had to think about that. "Fair point. A dog and a boy. This is going to be one interesting conversation with my mother."

My potential boyfriend was a thylacine. My

father was a canis lupus, and I was a combination of both worlds. This wasn't going to be easy, and it was so far from normal I wasn't sure what that word meant any more. Strangely, I didn't care.

Normal was overrated, anyway.

Glossary

000 = emergency number (911)

Biscuits = Cookies

Bitumen = Asphalt

Bugger = informal expletive which doesn't mean the formal dictionary meaning in Australia. It can mean:
1. A silly or annoying person. (Some bugger will have eaten it by tomorrow)
2. Something that is difficult or annoying (That tin is a bugger to open)
3. Used to denote sympathy. (That poor bugger)
4. Used to denote affection. (Cute little bugger)

Carpark = Parking lot

Cattle dog = Australian Shepherd

Chips = Chipped vegetables, usually potatoes. Can be used interchangeably to refer to fries or crisps.

Cordial = Fruit syrup which is then diluted with cold water to make a drink. Similar to 'Mio Liquid Water Enhancer' but with all the sugar and calories of Kool-Aid

Crockery = plates, dishes, cups, and other similar items, especially ones made of earthenware or china.

Cuppa = 'Cup of'. It usually refers to a hot drink. Tea, coffee, hot chocolate, soup etc.

Dag = an informal, non-offensive term meaning idiot

Dob = to report someone as for a misdemeanour. To tell an authority on someone

Dogsbody = generally someone who does drudge work, similar to a gofer, grunt or lackey.

Dump shop = similar to a thrift-store but located at the dump, where rummaged items in good condition are sold.

Fringe (of hair) = bangs

Jug (Kettle) = a container or device in which water is boiled, having a lid, spout, and handle, commonly electric.

Jumper = Sweater

Keen = Very interested

Having me on = to persuade someone that something is true when it is not, usually as a joke

Hospitality class = A subject at school based around the hospitality / tourism industry. It would be taken if the student is interested in a career as a Chef, Travel agent, Event Coordinator, Tour guide etc.

Lounge room = Living room

Mince = ground meat. Mostly beef, but can refer to any animal (turkey, pork, chicken etc.)

Pademelon = a small marsupial, similar in shape to a Kangaroo or Wallaby but smaller in size. Males of the species grow to about 7kgs (15lbs) and females are about half that.

Rubbish = trash

Stunned mullet = dazed; in complete bewilderment or astonishment

Takeaway = Takeout

Tea towel = Dish towel

Thick-shake = similar to a milk-shake but with ice cream added

Thylacine = (Also known as Tasmanian Tiger) Carnivorous marsupial native to Australia, presumed extinct.

Torch = Flashlight

Ute = Utility Truck / Pick Up Truck

Ute Tray = the bed of the Utility Truck

Ugg boots = A brand of Australian sheep skin, wool lined, slipper in the style of a boot, worn similarly to moccasins

Extinct

Shattered

"How did you die?"
"I didn't."

Sebastian Ashcombe has been trapped behind the mirrors of Ashcombe Manor almost 150 years. He can view the manor using the mirrors as windows to the solid world but he can't communicate with anyone and no one can see him

Until Now

Mattie Holmes visits Ashcombe Manor in Dunmore, England, after her mother marries Alex Ashcombe. The last thing she expects is a man in the mirror. Bastian is not a ghost. He didn't die. He was cursed behind the mirror on his wedding day in 1869. As they start to unravel the mystery they realise they are running out of time. If they don't break the curse before February 29th Bastian will simply disappear.

Breaking a centuries old curse is hard enough, but Mattie is starting to fall for Bastian. Not only is his very existence in jeopardy but to love a man in the mirror may only lead to a shattered heart.

"The story was a roller-coaster ride of emotions and I didn't see the plot twists coming."

"Fabulous multi-layered mystery."

Nova (Nephilim Code #1)

Nephilim walk among us. Descendants of Angels who just want to live their lives without humans knowing they exist. Some of them anyway. Then there are the ones who want to rule over us. Like in the days of old, they want to be considered our 'gods'.

My name is Nova Quinn. I'm a photographer…and human.

Well, I was.

Now I'm fighting for my life. I wasn't supposed to survive but I did. Caught in a world where 'superhuman' abilities are normal, it's hard enough trying to get a grip on this new reality. But when the other side shows up and wants to use my genetics for their experiments, suddenly it's no longer enough to know Nephilim exist – I have to be one.

My name is Nova Quinn.
And I'm the created Nephilim.

"Captured my whole attention by the second page and I couldn't put it down."

"Great combination of action, humour, intrigue, good vs evil and a wee bit of romance brewing."

Edward (Nephilim Code #2)

Nephilim once ruled this world and they are going to do so again. It's only a matter of time. The Rogues had better get on board or get out of the way.

Being Nephilim is my birthright but it was taken from me. Stripped of my abilities and disowned I have to face life in the human world. Then I meet the Rogues and things start looking up. I've found, not one, but both of the Nephilim Ibira Corp wants. Now, all I need to do is get them to trust me.

Getting their trust is a double-edged sword and there's more going on than I first realised. Discoveries and changes are just the beginning.

My name is Edward Huber.
And I've got a choice to make.

_____

"Exceptional character switch, absorbing story"

"I hated Edward in Book 1, but we see another side and he has become a very interesting character. I want more."

Zeph (Nephilim Code #3)

Nephilim are descended from Angels. Everyone knows the Angels died out eons ago. But not all Nephilim believe that. My grandfather didn't, and neither does my brother.

After the search for the Angel brings us to Australia, rumours arise that Ibira Corp has found the body of an Angel. They want it for its DNA. When they find out that we're on the trail of a live Angel, they'll go to great lengths to find him first.

Including harming our family.

With time running out and Ibira Corp not far behind, suddenly we're in a race to decipher the clues.

Discoveries and changes are just the beginning.

My name is Zeph Angelis.
And I've got an Angel to find..

"Fantastic book. Zeph had it all. Action packed. It had me crying, it made me laugh out loud, and there was even a developing romance."

"The author did an amazing job, with twists that I didn't see coming, to an ending that has me gasping."

Extinct